Also by the author:

The Yemenite Girl
Passion in the Desert
The Man Who Thought He Was Messiah
Partita in Venice
Diary of an Adulteress Woman
Ladies and Gentlemen, The Original Music of the Hebrew Alphabet and *Weekend in Mustaria (two novellas)*
A Novel of Klass
Zix Zexy Ztories
King of Yiddish
Kafka's Son
Kat or Cats: or, How Jesus Became My Rival in Love

ME, MO, MU, MA & MOD

Or, Which Will It Be,
Me and Mazal, or Gila and Me?

a true fiction

Curt Leviant

Livingston Press
The University of West Alabama
Livingston, Alabama

Library of Congress Control Number 2021945747

Printed in the United States
Publishers Graphics
Hardcover binding: HF Group

Typesetting and page layout: Joe Taylor, McKenna Darling
Proofreading: Kaylnn Ward, Joe Taylor, Caitlin Saxton,
Brooke Barger, Claire Banberg
Cover Design: Nic Nolin & Joe Taylor

Livingston Press is part of The University of West Alabama,
and thereby has non-profit status.
Donations are tax-deductible.

First edition
654321

ME, MO, MU, MA & MOD

Or, Which Will It Be,
Me and Mazal, or Gila and Me?

This book is dedicated to
Joe Taylor
my long time editor
and publisher
with affection
and esteem

Prolegomenon

Dear Mr. L,

In honor of 500 years of Jewish life in Venice, and as part of our celebration of this special anniversary, the Committee on the Arts of the Jewish Venice Quincentenary is awarding residency fellowships in Venice, commencing next June 1, to artists in various disciplines.

Since our Committee is familiar with your work, we are pleased to offer you an appointment as a Venice Fellow. This one-month writing fellowship includes round trip air fare and a beautiful, large, furnished apartment in a palazzo near St. Mark's Square.

For your part, in accepting, you agree to create a work inspired by the Jewish Quarter of Venice. If this appointment interests you, please write to the undersigned.

Once you have a project in mind, please send us your brief outline no later than one month prior to arriving. Be assured that as an artist you have complete freedom of expression, even to the point of changing your subject, should you so wish. The only immutable part is Jewish Venice as a subject or as background to your writing.

Other people in the arts have also been invited, but you are among the handful of writers chosen. We hope to hear from you soon.

Sincerely,
Samuele Ottolenghi
For la Comunità Ebraica di Venezia

PS Once you come, please do not be surprised at not finding me in Venice. I have to be in London during June, but I hope we can meet another time.

Dear Signor Ottolenghi,

I am honored by your invitation to become a Venice Fellow, which I accept gladly. I thank you for considering me and for giving me this appointment. Venice is one of my favorite cities and, as you may know, it is the setting of one of my novels. (Perhaps you or another member of your committee read Partita in Venice, *and this may have prompted your invitation.)*

As you may know, I teach Creative Writing and World Literature at Sage University and I am free during the months of June-August, so your proposed date is excellent timing.

In any case, even before I received your kind invitation, I had been thinking — for a forthcoming work of fiction — of choosing a noted Venetian Jew and telling his story.

As soon as I have something more definite I will write to you. Of course it will deal with Jewish Venice, but whether it will be a novel, novella, or long short story I do not know and probably will not know until I start writing.

I am sorry I won't be able to see you, Signor Ottolenghi, for I am familiar with your family name. Your distinguished countryman, Primo Levi (who, alas, ended his life before getting the Nobel Prize he deserved), married an Ottolenghi, no doubt a member of your family, and I know that the Ottolenghis are one of the old and renowned Jewish families in Italy.

Again I thank you for your letter. I look forward to spending some time in your beautiful, enchanting city.

Sincerely yours,

CL

Dear Signor Ottolenghi,

In the intervening weeks since I responded to your kind invitation, my head has been buzzing with the idea of writing about Jewish Venice and a subject has slowly been developing.

Here is my plan, subject of course to possible changes, as your letter of invitation indicated.

I was thinking about the fascinating late 16th century Leone da Modena, who was born in Venice, spent time there as rabbi, and is buried in the Jewish cemetery in the Lido, along with other luminaries.

As his unique autobiography tells us, he was a man of many professions, rabbi, author, musician, writer of comedies, even gambler. Indeed, his life seems to call for fictional treatment, especially since he is an enigmatic and occasionally controversial figure.

A story about this riveting Venetian Jew almost writes itself.

I want to add that there cannot be a better place for a writing fellowship than Venice. If there is magic in this world, magic that does not disappear with the blink of an eye, it is this city, with its fabled aura of quiet, its canals, gondolas, palazzi, Piazza San Marco, and the historic Ghetto with its seven synagogues which, miraculously, survived the German occupation.

And, so then, soon I will be in Venice, where the project will unfold.

With best wishes,

CL

PREFACE

I look up over the Venice Ghetto roofs and see — once, and maybe never again — in the azure sky, the cloudless Adriatic blue silk sky, a lone large gray bird with white fuzz above its tiny sad eyes, casually paddling its wings, backwards, as if it were an experimental flying machine created by Leonardo da Vinci, lazily paddling, and gazing at the airspace it had just traversed.

1 Discovery near the Synagogue

That slanted finger-length indentation I had seen on a stone doorpost in the famous Ghetto of Venice began it all.

It was a place for a mezuza on the right side of a hewn stone doorpost, a kind of fossil of a mezuza, a space that showed a once-upon-a-time mezuza. A space that cried out: the parchment with the prayer, Hear O Israel, is no longer here. Where is my mezuza?

But this may be a bit romanticized, heightened for maximum effect, for the dream of it.

Here's the story:

One day I was strolling on a side street in the Venice Ghetto. Remarkably, tourists just walk through the portal at the entrance to the Ghetto, marvel at the sign to the right of the entrance: Porto del Getto (yes, written there without an "h") and then continue on to Piazza San Marco. Curiosity doesn't pull them, as it does me. Wherever a little calle, I'm drawn, pulled, can't resist, as if I, or it, were a magnet.

That calle was near the main synagogue, which impressed me with its history, continuity and sanctity. As I walked on that little side street, eyes wide open, I noticed a house with that indentation. A few years back I had discovered something similar in two small houses in Girona, Spain (the home town of Nachmanides, the renowned thirteenth century Torah commentator and communal leader), just north of Barcelona. This indicated that a Jewish family had lived there before 1401, after which year Jews were no longer permitted to live in the environs of Barcelona. That the house had stood, unchanged, for more than six hundred years is another miracle.

At the door of that house in Venice, in that little calle near the main synagogue, I raised my fist to knock, then held back, thinking: What impertinence, intruding on a stranger's privacy just to satisfy my interest in Jewish matters. And then I thought: If I don't knock I may miss a fascinating story and I may regret my politesse. As these thoughts were chasing each other like melodies in a fugue I knocked before I had a chance to change my mind.

I waited a minute, got no response, and had already turned to leave, when the door opened. I saw before me a short, slightly built man wearing an old-fashioned cap, a white, open collar short-sleeved shirt and beige slacks. He had a little beard and appeared to be in his mid-thirties. Mid-thirties, yes, but still there was something old about him — the strands of white in his beard, the little crinkles at the sides of his brown eyes, and his mottled facial skin. With his head covered and his beard he appeared to be an observant Jew.

I greeted him with Shalom and a few words in Italian. Actually, he didn't have to be Jewish. Many men have beards and wear a cap. And just because he lived in a house that had a centuries-old indentation of a mezuza, why should I assume he was a Jew?

But he responded amicably with a Hebrew, "*Shalom u-verakha*," said a few words in Italian, then asked if I understood English. I said, Yes. As soon as he began to speak I heard a foreign lilt to his words, the music of Spanish in his English words.

I apologized for disturbing him and told him I was intrigued by that mezuza space on his doorpost, for I had seen something

Curt Leviant

similar in Spain.

"Girona, no doubt, where Nachmanides lived. I saw that there too."

His knowing this rather arcane fact surprised me. "That's exactly where I saw it," I told him. "And what a thrill it was walking on the same street on which this great man had walked. And that little angled finger-size depression in the stone where a mezuza had once been touched me. Said many silent words to me. And I am moved now too."

"Come in, come in," he said. "I see I have met a simpatico man." Then he stretched out his hand, shook mine warmly, and said, "My name is Mo."

I introduced myself and wondered how strange it was that this European had a typical American Jewish name from the 1920's — Mo.

As if reading my thought, he said, "As you just heard, my name is pronounced with a short European 'o', and not long like the American word for 'so' or 'go'."

Probably short for Moshe, I mused. But since he didn't offer to explain I didn't ask further. Then I thought: Mo is also the first syllable of Modena, the Venetian rabbi I wanted to write about. What an interesting confluence.

"Mo. Modena," I couldn't help exclaiming.

"No, no," he said. "No connection. But what makes you say that?"

"Well, I'm planning to write some kind of narrative about this famous man who was born here, served as rabbi here, and died here."

"Leone da Modena? The gambling rabbi, huh? Matchmaker, parodist, ghost writer? Probably every facet of his life makes for good fiction."

"Imagine! A rabbi, a card player. Strange combination. So you know Modena?"

Fact is, I was jealous. I thought no one knew about him. I didn't want anyone else to know about him. Somehow I wanted to have Modena all to myself.

"Leone da Modena? Of course I know him."

"What do you mean you know him? He lived some four hundred years ago."

Mo laughed. It was a laugh from his mouth, not his eyes.

"I mean, in a manner of speaking. I know his fascinating autobiography. When you read a well-written autobiography you get to know a man. I tell you, anyone acquainted with the development of Hebrew literature should know him. So you're a writer? Very impressive."

"Imagine!" I wanted to tell Mo something he probably didn't know. "At two-and-a-half he chanted the Haftora in the synagogue."

"He mentions this too in his autobiography, but go believe it. It's probably all self praise. There he also claims that at age three he read and explained Torah verses to a group of people. You can't believe anyone with anything. Not with fiction, not with non-fiction."

"Then what can you believe?"

"Poetry."

For a moment we looked at each other. Then Mo said:

"But you've chosen an ideal, certainly a fascinating, subject. Good luck with it."

I made a slight obeisance with my head that signaled thanks.

I regarded Mo closely. Did he notice my magnifying-glass eyes scanning his thin face, which was pinched just below both cheeks? I now saw that the beard served as a mask to hide pockmarks and scattered whitish discolorations, as if lentil-sized areas of his face had been bleached. Other tiny blemishes marked his forehead, cheeks and chin; perhaps he also had had papules once that were smoothed away by medication or a surgeon's scalpel. And this is why he no doubt had a little beard — to distract the eye.

During a moment's silence I looked around and saw there was little furniture in the room — an easy chair, a small writing desk, an inkwell and a quill — a quill? Now that's unusual, perhaps for decoration — some sheets of paper filled with hand-written lines, and a waist high bookcase. Then Mo lifted his chin — a polite way of saying, What is it you wish? Or, why did you stop by here besides asking about the mezuza?

But I anticipated his gesture and said:

"Are you a member of the community here, Mo?"

"Not really. I'm here on a visit. And since it's a temporary residence, I'm sure you know that putting the tiny parchment with the *Sh'ma Yisrael* in the mezuza is not obligatory."

I waited for him to continue. But he did not tell me what he was doing in Venice. Looking at his cap, I asked:

"Did you choose to live near the synagogue because of the short walk to services?"

"No, I wouldn't say that," he said, seemingly with forced patience, as indicated not by the tone of voice but by a slight narrowing of the eyes and a twick of the lips. The question, Are you secular? bubbled at the edge of my tongue but I did not articulate it. I admit, when I replayed my questions objectively in my mind,

I saw that they could be annoying and a touch obstreperous.

"Yes, a traditional Jew goes to services," Mo said with a little smile, evidently to mitigate the effect of his earlier remark. "But I'm a loner. Then you might ask me, So why are you here? The answer is that I enjoy the ambiance of this place, especially the synagogue's history, its continuity, its sanctity."

Hearing the very three words that had earlier gone through my mind, chills ran over me. I was about to tell him this but felt it sounded odd. How could those three words, and in the same order too, that I had said to myself be uttered so precisely by this man standing before me? Had he read my mind, or are such thoughts common to people of similar feelings and sensitivities?

His attitude towards prayer and services also struck me as strange. However, I didn't want to provoke a person I had just met. Even though I don't go regularly to the synagogue, it seemed to me that only when Jews gather in shul does sanctity of place become palpable. Otherwise, it's just a building with history and continuity. But Mo, aside from one testy remark, seemed like a fine man. I did not want to introduce tension into the delicate amity that had been created the first few minutes of our encounter.

But then he concluded with a poetic touch:

"Sometimes I go into the synagogue when no one is there and then I feel all three words on the palms of my hands."

Mo spread his hands as if he were going to show me the words on his palms.

A moment later, it dawned on me there's another reason he doesn't go to services. Why didn't I think of that right away? But now it was so obvious. Things you forget and suddenly remember always play out as obvious. Mo didn't want people staring at him in shul. He was probably embarrassed by the little blotches on his face.

"Have you met people in the community?" I asked, sensing I was straining to make conversation.

"One or two," Mo said.

"Have your been here long?"

"About a month," he said, "and you?"

"I just arrived a few days ago."

We stood there in silence. I weighed, with some dismay, the banality of our last exchanges. Then, since there was nothing more to say, I thanked him and was about to bid him goodbye.

Then I realized I had one more question and it wasn't banal. I let it run across the screen of my mind once and concluded it wasn't just words cast into the air. Actually, Mo himself had given me the opening. I knew the question was personal and that he might refuse to answer. But I decided to risk it anyway.

"Reb Mo," I said. "I know you might consider this a strange, perhaps even invasive, question. But since you said before that I might ask you, So why are you here, I will ask it in a more metaphysical manner: if you don't mind, can you tell me what brought you here?"

"Of course," he said at once, then added cryptically. "There is a reason for everything." And Mo looked me straight in the eye and wherever else his penetrating medieval glance could enter. "But sometimes we don't know why we're here until we've been here."

Now I really bid him goodbye and went outside, trying to unravel the enigma of his remark. He had obviously been to Spain, and with the Spanish accent in his English he likely had lived or was raised there.

But then, just as one might expect in good fiction, I heard the door open and Mo called to me. He stood in the doorway and, as I turned to face him, he said:

"You know, when you ask yourself a question it doesn't have the same ring as when someone else asks you the same question. I answered you before as if I had asked myself the question. But when someone else asks that very question — with the exact same words — it has a different shape, feel, personality, ambiance. So I thought over your question, which isn't the same as my question..."

"Excuse me, Mo, for interrupting you, but I'd like to tell you that you have a poet's sensibility to words and thoughts."

He half closed his eyes and nodded in gratitude.

"So here is my answer: Sometimes fate determines one's place in the world, and one has little control over the choices. But, yes, there is a reason why I am here now and it will likely unfold during my visit."

But these words are as vague as his previous ones, ran through my mind. In fact, they repeat the same thought with slightly different words.

"But that sounds very bookish," Mo continued, "as though I'm a character floating between two pages and two tiny curved lines precede and postcede my remarks. So I will amend my remark to say only, yes, there is a reason why I'm here." And he raised his hand and made a scrubbing motion in front of himself as though wiping some letters off a chalkboard.

Not only didn't I understand his remarks, I had no real answer to my, our, his, question. And his gesture was even more puzzling. Did he want to hint that someone, something, would disappear?

Curt Leviant

In retrospect, it seemed to me we hadn't said much to each other in our brief encounter — but his pregnant thought that only poetry was credible was fixed in my mind — all of which began with my seeing a mezuza indentation in a door post made of stone more than five hundred years ago.

And I'm glad Mo didn't turn the tables on me and ask me why, I mean really really, why was *I* here?

2   In the Synagogue

Up near the roof and almost out of sight, except if you know where and how to look, in the interior of the ornate 16th century Sephardic synagogue in Venice, with its huge standing brass candelabras in front of the Holy Ark, old hand-wrought hanging chandeliers, and worn smooth dark mahogany seats, each with its own private reading desk, up up, way up, there is a women's gallery in the attic.

If you sit in the men's section downstairs you see it when you look up, way up, and there it is, floating almost, almost evanescent, full of seemingly endless old mahogany latticework. But that women's gallery is no longer used, for it is a steep climb, two more narrow flights up to the attic, and quite arduous for the elderly. Who knows what old footprints cling to the dusty boards, or what memories adhere to the wood or hover in the tiny square spaces between the crisscrossed wooden slats?

Now the women's section is downstairs, on the same level as and opposite the men's. Here the women are partially visible through similar wooden slats, for the slats are spaced farther apart.

Long ago, upstairs, the women were not only invisible; they were totally forgotten. But now, downstairs, with coming and going, standing and sitting, heads bent together, they make their presence felt. And if the woman is pretty, her aura wafts across the open space of the synagogue between the men's and women's sections, across the marble tiled floor, and insinuates itself into the seats where the men sit.

It was there, one Sabbath morning in that old synagogue, sitting opposite me, behind the not-so-impenetrable wooden partition, that I first saw this attractive, quiet woman with an oval face perfectly made. I saw at a glance — one look sufficed — a dolor about her eyes that made her look vulnerable; but this added to her attraction. She seemed to hover on the cusp of lonely and sad. Sometimes it is hard to tell one from the other.

By herself she sat, at a distance from the other women, who were clustered together.

I saw her holding the Siddur, the prayer book at which she glanced occasionally and sometimes turned the pages. Most of the time, however, she looked out, above and beyond, as though dreaming, but never at the men sitting opposite her. And I certainly didn't hear her singing the melodies that the other women knew.

New to Venice myself, I didn't know people well enough in the community to ask about her, a woman seemingly in her late thirties, who sat by herself and spoke to no one. For, like men, women too chat in the women's gallery, their heads almost touching as they speak. But not this woman. I imagined her new to the tightly knit and closed Venetian Jewish community. And no wonder they are so self-contained. It is hard to befriend visitors if every *Shabbat* a new group of fifty-sixty tourists comes on Friday night and vanishes Saturday at noon.

I tried to imagine who she was. Since she didn't cover her hair she probably wasn't married. Perhaps she was a widow from Lombardy or a divorcee from Pisa; perhaps her husband had left her (why anyone would leave her is a mystery). Maybe she had suffered a tragedy and needed to be alone. Or perhaps someone in her family had died and, as is natural, people move away from the proximity of death as from the plague, even though in the Jewish tradition comforting the bereaved is a duty, and, as it is written in the sacred texts: he who comforts a mourner takes away 1/60th of his grief.

At the same time, with the contrapuntal thoughts the mind is capable of, something akin to singing harmony with yourself, I imagined other people who hadn't spoken to me either, wondering who I was, where I had come from, and what I, neither a divorcee from Pisa nor a widow from Lombardy, was doing in Venice.

While I was praying, an odd thing happened: in one of the lines I saw a comma in the text separating two words. But when I looked again it seemed to have disappeared. I read further down the page, ascribing this to a trick of the eye or to the light. But I was drawn back — curiosity is such a powerful mover — to the top of the page and there it was, the comma that had presumably vanished.

But it turned out that this momentarily missing comma was just a foreshadowing — I'm dying to use the word adumbrate, but I resist — for what would happen later: a semi-colon in my printed Siddur left the page and floated up a few inches. To make sure I was seeing properly, I held the Siddur horizontally at eye level, the edge of the book touching the middle of my nose. And there it was, that little semi-colon, solid, tiny, obviously three-dimensional, dangling in the air, like a little hook, inches above the page. To call attention to itself, that period, and beneath it a comma, both were a shiny, polished ink black.

I looked about; didn't want people staring at me. I put the Siddur down. Blinked. Looked to my left and to my right. Closed my eyes. Wished away the little phantasmagoria and off it went.

But when I re-opened the Siddur to the affected page that semi-colon was still there.

Then the question arises. When isn't there a question? If a punctuation point rises up from a page, why a semi-colon? Had it been a period alone, it wouldn't have been so readily seen. An exclamation point is too loud, too attention grabbing. But what about a question mark? Now that's a good question. A question mark would elicit philosophical speculation. Why is it there? What question is being asked? What problem is nigh that has to be solved? But an innocent semi-colon doesn't convey much; has little to say. A dangling, floating, off-the-page semi-colon just indicates there are matters here that go beyond the mundane. But since there is a reason for everything, there was even a reason for that, which I discovered soon enough.

Then I remembered; I had read about something similar in a novel, *King of Yiddish*, some years back. The protagonist was bathing in his tub and, seemingly from the tiled wall, the first three Hebrew letters of the word Yiddish, *yud, yud, daled*, about half an inch in size, materialized, hung in the air and, as the man was about to grasp them, the letters slipped away and vanished. He too was in a world where dark energy collided with dark matter.

While musing thus in the synagogue, the sexton, seeing a new face, called me up to the Torah. After my aliya, I exchanged a few words in Hebrew with the rabbi. His sabra accent indicated he was Israeli, and his darker skin showed that his family came from the Middle East. He was on the short side, carried himself erect, and had no beard, rather unusual for an Orthodox rabbi. His black hair was cut rather long, and the nostrils of his short nose had a dramatic little flare which accented his engaging good looks.

After Sabbath morning services, according to Venetian custom, the Chief (and only) Rabbi of Venice, speaking in English and Italian, invites everyone in shul to come to the courtyard in back of the community building, about a five-minute walk from the synagogue, and participate in a festive Kiddush, the traditional blessing recited over wine, followed by a variety of savory and sweet snacks.

No, I had not seen Mo at the Sabbath services. I had looked for him but he was not there.

3 Kiddush in the Courtyard

Under an arched blue tarpaulin cover, supported by chrome poles, stand three long tables covered with white plastic tablecloths bedecked with various salads on larger plates. Smaller plastic plates, forks and napkins are scattered along the three tables. A couple of women offer tiny plastic cups filled with wine. The rabbi holds a goblet of wine, chants the Kiddush, and drinks; only then do the people begin to serve themselves.

I looked at the faces of the women gathered around the table; there must have been twenty or so, but I did not see the pretty woman with the sad face I had noticed earlier. But then I spotted her moving away from the tables to an empty chair further back in the courtyard near an old chestnut tree. She had a slightly unsure walk, wooden might be a good term, like a new-born lamb, as though she had only recently learned to stand on her legs.

She sat by herself — once more by herself — eating demurely. Whereas everyone here was chatting with someone else, to her no one drew near. I wanted to approach and speak to her, but because I was an outsider I held back.

I noticed that the rabbi, who had previously been talking to someone, was now free.

I went up to him, wished him *Shabbat shalom*, and added in Italian:

"Would you mind if I asked you a question?"

"Oho, so you speak Italian. Are you a teacher?"

"No no, I just love the language."

"What's your profession?" the rabbi asked.

"I'm an American writer here on the Venice fellowship."

"Wonderful. Congratulations. So how can I help you?"

"I see the tourists mingling with the Venetians, but one person, that young woman over there, is all by herself. No one talks to her. Seems like a mystery."

"A guest for a while sees for a mile," he said in English, replaying the Yiddish proverb.

"How so?"

"You got it right. She is a mystery. And, true, no one talks to her."

Since the rabbi had given me such a cordial response, I continued:

"She seems to have a sadness etched into her face. It is as if her face is frozen into a serious, never-a-smile expression."

"Yes. You are very observant, a necessary writerly quality. Is this the first time you've seen her?"

"Yes. I just came a few days ago. This is my first *Shabbat* here."

"You're right," the rabbi said. "She is always alone. No one talks to her."

"That's so strange. But why?"

"Because they know her."

Now I know what an oxymoron is, but this one was slippery. Because they know her they don't speak to her. I felt that this mystery has to be unraveled, so I said:

"What does that mean?"

"Since they know she won't answer they don't talk to her."

"Is she angry at them for some reason? Has someone insulted her? Hurt her feelings?"

"No."

"Then why won't she answer?" I asked. "She looks like a fine but lonely woman."

"You see, it's rather simple. It seems she cannot speak," the rabbi said.

Why didn't he tell me that right away? Why stretch out this strange conversation? And more. Is her muteness a reason not to approach her or engage with her? These thoughts bubbled on my lips, but I held back from saying them aloud.

"But can she understand?"

"Apparently. She also keeps her distance, very likely because of her impediment. She doesn't encourage contact."

Seeing a couple near us who wanted to speak to the rabbi, I said, "*Shabbat shalom*, rabbi."

He shook my hand and said, "Call me Roni."

After my chat with the rabbi I walked to where the young woman was sitting. If no one talks to her, I decided, I will. My first view of her was in semi-profile. She wore a short-sleeved white blouse decorated with tiny roses scattered across the cotton fabric and had quite shapely legs, visible from between the suede black half boots and the bottom of her middle-length flared violet skirt.

She sat alone on a folding chair, next to a knee-high stone fence around the chestnut tree, one of the few trees in the enclosed courtyard. Venice, which is such a public place, with squares, lanes and alleys, but very few parks, has little private space. And this park-like courtyard was private. It shut Venice out from itself. She evidently enjoyed this privacy and was looking off into the distance, perhaps wondering about one of those high Ghetto "skyscrapers", six stories high, the tallest residential buildings in Venice.

I stood for a moment and rehearsed all kinds of remarks, including "Are you new here, like I am? And isn't this a wonderful place to be in?" Nothing profound, but surely phrases that would elicit some kind of response.

On her lap she held a plastic plate with egg salad, humus, and two burekas. As she ate I noticed her long, sensuous, elegant fingers, fingers that moved gracefully as her hand rose up to brush her long auburn hair away from her face.

I approached from the side and now saw her in full profile.

Looking at her close up I saw that this young woman with the oval face had a thin nose, pink lips and high cheekbones. And she was rather tanned, which I hadn't noticed before, and she wore no makeup. Then she turned. I said she was pretty, a prettiness tinged with sadness. But one might also add austere, perhaps even cold. Certainly the area around the mouth argued for this. But her kindly eyes said otherwise. When she caught me staring at her, the expression on her face mingled astonishment and startle, as if I had surprised her.

But the startle was all mine. For what I saw from the front had not been visible from the side. It was seen only when you faced her. For she had nonpareil eyes. Something I had heard about, perhaps read in a folk story, but never seen. She had eyes not black or brown, blue or green — but blue *and* green. Two differently-colored eyes: the left, lavender blue; the right, chartreuse green. Whoever created her had either made a fantastic mistake or a successful and daring experiment.

"*Shabbat shalom*," I said, my eyes dancing between one eye and the other. "Do you understand English?"

She indicated yes.

"I saw you in the synagogue before."

She nodded but did not smile.

"Are you new here, like me? I just arrived a few days ago."

She gave me a kind of angled nod that seemed to say, Welcome!

"I'm an American writer here for a month or so. Are you a member of the community here or are you a newcomer too?"

She ticked her head in an arc several times, as if to say, neither new nor old. Then, as if remembering that she had to make herself understood, she pointed to her lips and throat and wagged her forefinger.

I don't know why I didn't say the following words out loud. It's as if I had unconsciously taken on her manner and, unable to speak, I mouthed, "I understand."

I usually tell girls I meet that they have a melodic and mellifluous voice; for some reason they like to hear that. If melodic doesn't enchant them mellifluous does. But now that pat compliment was totally non apropos.

She pointed to her mouth, made a chewing motion, and then made a few stabbing motions toward me with her index finger. She was asking me why I wasn't eating?

"It's all right," I said. Then I told her my name and asked, "What's your name?"

Then something strange and memorable happened, something out of the storybook world, that same once-upon-a-time wherein you find a heroine with one eye lavender, the other chartreuse.

She suddenly took my left hand and with the tip of her elegant right forefinger, long as a musical note, made three tiny movements on my left palm as if she were writing something. At once, I felt an electric thrum, a spasm of current, a wave of desire, the beginning and shape of which I saw surging, roaring through my body the minute her quill finger touched me.

It wasn't an unpleasant shock, like sticking your finger into a live socket, or the sharp sensation when you sprain your ankle and the sudden stab of pain makes you cry out. On the contrary, it felt good, a thrill of vibration, much like what a taut string feels when a seasoned violinist draws his bow across it. It felt as if the essence of melody, the innate melody that each Hebrew letter possesses, had entered me, and I was vibrating with dense, compressed song.

At that moment I felt something new. As if an angel's wing had flown by me, and I sensed its silken tips brushing my skin. And the sudden warming — perhaps I should substitute an "n" for the "m" — on the palm of my left hand. Was it letters she had traced on my hand? The culture of people who cannot speak encouraged them to be more open with their feelings, to throw away reticence and restraint, which are the hang-ups of people who speak. And I fantasized that she had instantly been smitten with me and written three words,

I love you, in the palm of my hand, for as she was writing she looked up at me with a kindly, pleasant expression, but still no smile, a no smile that was a Mona Lisa smile.

Where she had touched me is one of the body's most sensitive areas. And it felt good, wonderful, ecstatic. And then I looked at my palm and saw she had written the three Hebrew letters for *Shabbat*, שבת *shin, bet, tav* from right to left, and I saw that the color of those three Hebrew letters was a subdued red. When her index finger touched my palm, I almost clasped my fingers around hers. But as soon as her index finger began to move, I raised my head and gazed up into the lavender sky, where I saw a big gray

Curt Leviant

bird with small sad eyes defying nature, flying backwards.

She pointed to the word she had written on my palm and waved her finger back and forth the way a mother indicates No No No to a child. Again she was telling me that it was the Sabbath and it was not permitted to write. Otherwise, she would have responded to my question and written her name.

Now there was another anomaly here. In order to inform me she does not write on *Shabbat* she was writing on *Shabbat*. Or was spelling out letters on one's skin akin to writing in the air; that is, not considered writing at all? And still one more, which I think of now as I write these lines, but about which I had never asked her: if she was already writing the word *Shabbat*, why couldn't she write her name? Or were there subtle differences in her religious portfolio that I wasn't aware of? Like answering a direct question was considered work, a violation of the Sabbath, but reminding someone that it was the Sabbath was not held as labor.

I must say, I cannot hide it, even if I wanted to hide it, I cannot hide it, for the letters are still still there, albeit a bit fainter, but still still there, the glow still there, these three Hebrew letters indited by the index finger of her right hand, glowing red on the palm of my left.

After she had imprinted that *Shabbat* into me there were times when I felt disoriented. As if a moment of forgetfulness had come over me. Not a headache, but an absence of a headache, as though I had exited from myself and only a bit of me remained. And I actually sensed a little flight within me, from my stomach upward, something intangible moved like a vortex up and out of me. Gone was my full awareness. It felt like a spell of dizziness, at which I stood still and took a deep breath, hoping to return to myself. But I did not lose my balance or succumb in any other way.

Still, for a moment, my senses were in disarray. Had you asked me my name I would have stared blankly. I did not know where I was, what month we were in, what day, the date. Although I felt removed, I knew that something had happened to me. My sense of time was suspended; this feeling lasted only seconds, but it seemed forever. A swirl of something, ineffable, invisible, turned in my head and also in my field of vision. And, more, that ever so slight pulse of letters in my left palm. Then I had the idea, as if someone had whispered it to me, of looking at the Hebrew letters, and I did what the mute woman had done before. She had touched my palm. And now so did I. And that was the magic elixir. Then the colorless fog, to give it a name, imprecise I know, because it was thicker than fog, more like a triple layer of it, with the density of a light fabric, but that momentary removal of myself from myself lifted and I was back to what I was, what I had been. Again the battle between dark energy and dark matter.

But I still did not know her name.

How fascinating she is, flew through my mind. How can I fit this unusual woman into my Leone da Modena story? Introduce her to Mo? What a strange couple they would be.

At once I had an idea. The entire scene appeared before me. Modena, at a card game with one of the wealthiest Jews in Venice, keeps losing. He sees the man's beautiful daughter standing on the side, watching; he wonders if she might somehow be signaling the cards to her father. But then the tables turn and Modena starts winning one game after another. The rich man is almost broke. "I can't play anymore," he says, "because I can't pay any more." Modena looks at the beautiful daughter and has an idea.

Modena isn't the only guy with ideas.

I looked at the real, not the imaginary, beautiful woman before me. She seemed out of an earlier era. Not that there was anything old about her. Not at all. But just like you can look at an Old Master portrait and gauge the time zone not by the clothing but by the face, the same could be done with her. Her face, her walk, her silence were part of a pre-modern bundle. I bet if she could speak one would conclude there was a medieval patina to her voice too.

Then, on the top stone of the fence around the chestnut tree, the mute woman with the vulnerable sadness on her pretty face rested in vertical position her forefinger and middle finger. And she moved them slowly forward, walking with her fingers.

I looked around. No one was paying attention to us. The synagogue crowd was gathered around the table, still helping themselves to the prepared foods.

She saw me looking and tapped me on the hip, as if to say, Pay attention to me and not to the crowd. Again she made that little walking motion with her two fingers and pointed to herself and to me.

I brightened. "Sure," I said.

She held up her hands, asking me to wait for another message. Now she pointed to herself and to the exit. She spread her fingers, palms downward and moved her hands up and down gently three times, signaling have patience. With eyes widened she pointed to me and to the exit and again made that two-finger walking motion.

"I understand," I said softly. "First you go and then a couple of minutes later, I will leave."

She nodded. She didn't want our exit to attract attention.

I don't know if she smiled, but I noticed that the previous built-in tristesse on her face had eased somewhat.

I don't want to give the impression that she was a thorough-going innocent. Despite her muteness, she was not. In fact, that disability seemed to sharpen, strengthen, her sight and hearing and her cerebral skills.

Once we were outside, away from the entrance to the community building, she took my hand again, and pointed to the word she had impressed onto my skin. She arched and pointed her forefinger in a bow-like motion that indicated "next". Once more that touch of hers sent a delicious vibrato through me, a pleasant turmoil neatly tied with a tiny red ribbon of pain.

"Next *Shabbat*?" I asked.

She said Yes with her head.

"No. No. I don't want to wait until next *Shabbat*. Why not today? I thought we were going to walk today."

I strained my ears in vain to hear the wordless sound a person would make when saying No, something like "n-n, n-n." But such a sound did not come out of her throat.

She wagged her finger.

"You can't today, is what you're saying."

She nodded.

"How about tomorrow? You see, if we meet on a weekday, you can write also."

She touched the *Shabbat* on my palm, not realizing the turmoil her touch caused me. She made a sign for plus, then raised her index finger to signal one.

"The Sunday following next *Shabbat*?"

She indicated Yes with her head.

I looked again at the word she had imprinted on my palm.

I turned to see if people were coming out of the community building. They were evidently still eating, for no one was emerg-

Curt Leviant

ing from the main door. But by the time I turned back to her she had disappeared. The trouble was that from where we stood there weren't too many calles she could have slipped away into.

Darn it, why didn't I agree to meet her next *Shabbat*? Now I had nothing. Now I would have to wait eight days to start this adventure all over again.

Thinking of what had just happened with this alluring unicum woman, I realized that my plan of bringing her in as a romantic interest for Modena, while engaging at first, was already starting to fade. Quickly come, quickly go. She overshadowed him; no doubt about it, her presence overwhelmed his. She was real, here, while Modena was a figure from the past, interesting but vague, more imagined than real. Instead of seeing Modena through a pair of binoculars I was regarding him now from the other end of a telescope.

Nevertheless, Leone da Modena's fascinating image was still there, not completely gone.

4   Meeting a Runner

A couple of days later, as I strolled on one of my favorite streets, Via Garibaldi, the widest street in Venice, a runner stopped in front of me. He wore a gray baseball cap and a black and white jogger's outfit with a long fish-shaped splash of yellow on his black t-shirt.

"Shalom," he said.

At first I didn't recognize him.

"It's me, Roni, the rabbi," he said in English, greeting me cheerfully as if I were an old friend.

"You, Roni, a runner?" I couldn't help express my astonishment.

"I do a five-mile run every morning except *Shabbat*."

"So nice to see a rav doing this. And so unusual too."

"Well, I don't fit into the usual rabbinic mold."

I could see at once that he didn't.

"How many rabbis do you know who speak six languages?" he said proudly.

"Six? Which ones?"

"Hebrew, my native language. English, Italian, French, Spanish and Arabic."

"That's quite impressive. You studied them in college?"

"Never went....Tell me," he said, running in place like a practiced jogger, "are you still going to be here for *Shabbat*?"

"Yes, Roni, I'll be here for a few more weeks."

"Fine, so would you like to come for Friday night dinner at my apartment?"

"A pleasure. That'd be wonderful. Thank you so much for the invitation."

"I live in the community building. First door to your right, upstairs. The same main entrance you use when you come to the courtyard for the *Shabbat* Kiddush."

"Yes, I know exactly where it is."

"So you will walk home with me on Friday night after davenning."

I smiled. "I like the way you, you're obviously not an Ashkenazi, use the Yiddish word for praying."

"By now that word is international. I've even seen it in the *New York Times*, without italics, and without explanation. So I guess it's now a standard English word."

"And where is your perfect English from?"

"My father was born in Aden, a British colony in south Yemen, and English was the basic language. Of course, the Jews spoke Hebrew and knew Arabic too." Roni stopped for a moment, then added, "And your writing? Going well? I hope you're finding inspiration here."

"Venice is the perfect place for stories and adventure," I said somewhat evasively.

I wasn't prepared to talk about it, but a little aesthetic agitas was simmering in me: the Leone da Modena project in nervous tremor. At first I had had a great idea: elide the attractive mute woman into a Modena adventure. But then I realized it was false. False and forced. She was far more interesting. You know the old saying, present overrides past. But yet, but yet — somehow I couldn't totally shake Leone da Modena from my consciousness. This man with dozens of professions still had something going for him. Good, Roni's eyes seemed to say. And then the running rabbi took off.

5 Venice Rav and Mazal

The next Friday night in the synagogue I looked for the mute young woman but did not see her. There was a tweak in my heart as I saw that empty space and tried to fill it.

I gave a quick look at the palm of my left hand. Still there, that inscribed three-letter Hebrew *Shabbat.* Were the letters indeed real or was it my imagination? Nothing is real until it is confirmed by another person. But I didn't want to risk the embarrassment of asking someone a possibly ridiculous question:

Excuse me, but do you see some Hebrew letters here on the palm of my hand?

Or rather, something more neutral:

Can you see something here on my palm?

But I consoled myself with the hope that I'd see her again, if not at the Sabbath morning service then surely for the Kiddush in the courtyard. For how could we confirm our date for Sunday if I didn't see her on *Shabbat*?

I had expected more people at the rabbi's Friday night dinner. But there were only three of us — all men. Roni, Professor Umberto dei Rossi, who taught medieval philosophy at the Universita di Roma, and I. When I remarked that dei Rossi is a noted Jewish Italian name, he said, Yes; he came from one of the old Roman Jewish families who traced their lineage back to pre-Christian, Roman times.

After Kiddush over wine, we began with various salads that

the rabbi himself had made. Just then we heard knocking. Roni jumped up to go to the door. I heard a woman's voice. My heart leaped; then a quickened beat. It's her. She's coming for supper. Roni, bless him, perhaps reacting to my question about her, had decided to break her isolation and bring her into the community. I felt her three-lettered Shabbat שׁבּ warming my palm. The rest of me was warming too. But the merry chirping at the door-way pricked my fantasy as I remembered she was mute. The new-comer, a girl in her mid-twenties, came in with a bright, "*Shabbat shalom.*" Soon as I saw her my own *Shabbat* responded with a pulse.

There's nothing like a late entrance to make you look up and take notice. And the first thing, well, maybe the second, you noticed about her was her big yearning, dreamy eyes. It seemed it was they who had swept into the room. Her long, slightly up-curved dark eyes, so mesmerizing were they, I couldn't even recall their hue at first glance. That's what caught you, those eyes, hooking everyone who looked at her and look they did — stopping in mid-bite, even mid-swallow — the eyes dancing, she fully aware that they were dancing, welcoming, teasing, tugging at you to make you fix your attention on her.

For beauty and allure alone do not suffice. Beauty has to have a mirror. And that's what we, the admirers, were. All this in a moment's glance; quicker than an eye blink. Certainly less than it takes to write these lines.

I hadn't noticed a couple of extra plates and some cutlery at the edge of the table. Since Roni hadn't prepared a place setting for her, I guess he wasn't sure if she would come. Soon as she sat down somehow the magic of her eyes faded. The eyes, see supra, now I saw they were brown, with little flecks of orange dotted within, were the second thing you noticed about her. Here's the first, and this is why one lost interest for a while in her eyes.

She was short, about five-three or five-four, and just a whit on the plump side, was the newcomer, call it delectable plump, with a round pretty face — an innocence radiated from it — and heavily made up, at least around the eyes. She wore what she thought was a demure white long-sleeved blouse, but it was low cut and the tanned top of her breasts were seen. Her cleavage was so deep it could have housed two lusty, lactose tolerant little fellas. Not the sort of attire one would see in an Orthodox synagogue or in a rabbi's house. In fact, she had not been at the synagogue for the just-concluded Evening Service, where only a handful of women attended. And I was aware of each one, you may be sure, not for their presence but for the absence of the mute pretty woman with one eye lavender, the other chartreuse, I had hoped to see.

The girl who had come in had a yellow sash tight around her waist that accented her boobs all the more. They — you know what the pronoun refers to — there was no gainsaying it, no way around the remark, they, like her eyes were also eye-catching, attention-grabbing. And all six male eyes, including the rabbi's, did just that.

At the sight of those two "grand tetons" (her phrase, not mine, as you will soon see), especially when she walked and those two bounties bounced up and down, fuzzed away were all thoughts of Friday night table hymns in praise of the Creator and His gift of Sabbath repose to His people Israel. She even made me forget the mute woman with the unforgettable multi-colored eyes whose name I still did not know, who had written *Shabbat* in three Hebrew letters on the palm of my left hand that I could not forget because the letters throbbed there in a rhythm.

But, unlike rigorously observant (or ultra-Orthodox) Jewish girls who wear a loose-fitting buttoned sweater or a jacket to deflect attention from their chests, she chose an array of clothing that focused rather than reduced attention. From the yellow sash down my memory is weak. I think she had on a rather short gray skirt and pantyhose, following the habit of Orthodox Jewish girls who never wear slacks but only dresses or skirts.

She seemingly knew the rabbi, for she did not introduce herself to him when she came in, but addressed Umberto and me: "*Mon nom est Mazal.*"

Even though we were in Venice , first she spoke French, but seeing that one of us — me! — could barely understand her, she began with a halting Hebrew. In this language her remarks were muddled. Every other word sounded like an incomprehensible *utaine* and *qomu*, a kind of backward Aramaic. Neither I nor the rabbi understood her. And then, out of consideration for the philosophy professor, who knew no Hebrew, we asked her if she spoke English. She said, "Yes, a small."

Mazal's English was indeed small, and not at all like Shakespeare's "small Latin, less Greek", in Ben Jonson's memorable phrase. If you measured her English by clothing size it was below small and just above petite. In fact, it was a picturesque Frenglish. But at least in this language we understood a bit more although not everything she was trying to tell us. She was from Paris, she said; but her name, Mazal, indicated that her family stemmed from Morocco. She said she had studied a bit of Hebrew and taught young children in a synagogue's religious school in Paris.

"Are you here for a vacation?" I asked her.

"Not in realitay. I have large passion desire," and here she closed her eyes prayerfully for a moment, "go to Padua visit bury space of middle evil Spanish rabbi with name, the Maitre de Padua, Rav Moses. He possess fame name to bringing quarrel parties to coming..." She brought her hands together, fingertips touching. "So I passion desire visit his stone of tomb and pray and cry him to mix in quarrel what...." and here Mazal mimed tearing a piece of paper, "....moi synagogue in Paris and make tres grande problematique pour moi."

Mazal tried to tell us about what was tearing her shul apart and why she was seeking the help, the intervention, of the long-dead Rabbi Moses, the Master of Padua. But her excitation, even agitation, on this issue and her imperfect English made the words sound truncated, almost as inaccessible as her previous Hebrew. Like a poor connection on the telephone where every other word, or every other syllable was missing. So we gathered it was something with her and the congregation, but not exactly what. I think the word rabbi was in there somewhere but I couldn't tell if he was on her side, their side, our side, or no side.

So it left room for speculation, which is always more alluring than mere facts.

What had she done in Paris, I wondered, that prompted her to take this long pilgrimage to Venice and the Padua cemetery? And would a visit there give her a basket of necromantic, superstitiously tinged beneficence she could carry back to Paris to counteract the negative vibes that had been cast at her back home? Although Mazal had mentioned Paris a few times, I had a hunch she came from one of the poor suburbs where North African Jews tended to settle after coming to France decades ago.

And she was either vague about the details or couldn't properly express them. Her outline too was frayed at the edges and, coupled with her kitchen English, it was hard to follow her story with absolute certainty.

Umberto dei Rossi and I exchanged glances. Through our silence, with just a slight grimace, a raised eyebrow, twist of the lips, we shared our incredulity at her narrative.

I was a guest at the rabbi's house for the first time. Mazal was also a guest. What business did I have to butt in? I didn't know the girl. But I can't stand stupidity, especially when it's cloaked in religion. And superstition. So I could not restrain myself; the tumult in me overrode good breeding. Not that I didn't think about it. I did. Saul Bellow's novella, "The Bellarosa Connection", has a marvelous phrase about the benefit of silence when one is im-pelled to speak: "the hidden advantage of a buttoned lip." I tried to remember that trenchant phrase as I rushed headlong like a mis-fired torpedo into a harangue I shouldn't have begun, and in front of the local rabbi too.

"In the Torah, Moses, the real one, not the Italian or Spanish one, tells the Israelites that when they come to the Land of Isra-el, not to follow the abominations of the pagans. Not to practice witchcraft or sorcery. Not to do necromancy, as the Hebrew says, *doresh el ha-metim*, inquire of the dead. About this Moses says whoever does this does an abomination to God."

Mazal paled. That big word was the same in French, I guessed. Then, seeing her graying face, I lunged again:

"I hope you'll excuse me, Mazal, but how can an intelligent girl who professes belief in God indulge in kabbalistic voodoo by prostrating oneself on a grave of a Rabbi Moses dead probably more than three hundred years?"

I'm sure she didn't understand some of the words but she got the gist of my remark.

"First of everything," Mazal shot back, "can you able measure with ruler faith, belief? And two of everything, can you able measure what faith accomplishing?"

In retrospect, her reply was well thought out. But I couldn't stop.

"But Judaism is a religion of life, not death," I said. "The Torah and the prophets cry out against those who make a cult of death worship."

Mazal scowled. Or tried to. She slid her glance past me and Umberto to the rabbi. She looked at him, evidently hoping for some reaction. Then she said:

"For much century, juifs gone to cementaire. Outstretched on ancestor graves of holy mens, and passion beg them answer moi prayers."

I responded: "The greatest Sephardic authority, Moses Maimonides, also known as Rambam, was against going to graves. He was dead against it."

I looked at Umberto. He smiled at my little, admittedly inadvertent, pun.

"Jews who do that are influenced by their Christian surroundings," I continued. Oh, was I sailing, propelled by a self-created good head wind, I was sailing on a pulpit of my own creation. "The goyim pray to saints and ask them to intercede with God. That's not monotheism. That's idol worship. We don't need intercessors. We pray directly to God.... Do you know what intercessors are?"

"No," Mazal said, frowning. With her brow furrowed she suddenly seemed older.

"Middlemen....If you don't pray directly to God it's pagan."

Curt Leviant

"No. Is part juif tradition." Mazal fixed her big beautiful, or-ange-flecked, mesmerizing brown eyes on me. But I wasn't going to be bamboozled by her eyes or blindsided by her boobs.

"That still doesn't make it kosher. It still violates the spirit of monotheism. Monotheism doesn't go for superstition, presen-timents, *mazal*, despite your name which you know means luck or star, it doesn't go for conjunction of stars, takes no stock in a propitious hour. That said, I have to reverse what I just said and say: But Jews, even traditional juifs, do just that. They shouldn't but they do. Witness the Hebrew expression, *siman tov* and *mazal tov* — which means a good sign and a good conjunction of stars. And the Yiddish expression: *in a guteh shaw* — in a propitious hour. Like sex, the allure of such easy belief is too hard to resist."

At mention of that elemental monosyllable up she perked. At the very least, there was some kind of gut reaction; a little sudden forward thrust of her torso; and a flush, a flash of color, on Mazal's face. Maybe her ears turned red.

She caught her breath and sighed.

For a while she was quiet. I thought I had won. And then:

"My rabbi teach moi that great Sephardi wise man, ibn Ezra, in commentary on Book Exodus, he writes, places on earth they change accordion to *mazal* what is over them" — and here Mazal smiled — "the mazal you mention, the star what has power on them, and ibn Ezra he say wise astrologia mens will overstand this."

If she'd been blessed with but the slightest smidgen of sophis-tication, just one avoirdupois ounce of it, she could have looked at me, through me, with utter disdain, with chill indifference, then turned to the rabbi with a smile and said something banal like, "You chicken delicious." With one stroke she could have demolished my attack. Such ill-disguised contempt would have stopped me dead cold. But her responses egged me on. She didn't have the power of silence, the skill of buttoned lip. And neither did I.

For I said:

"It is all the more pitiable, Mazal, that your Paris rabbi believes this and even that a great commentator like ibn Ezra believed this. They couldn't resist superstition. It's so sad that juifs who believe in one God also believe in the roulette wheel of constellations. And I can never overstand why some pious Jews think this way. Believers in superstitions are affected by two words that sound the same: they are wrapped in a veil of ignorance and they live in a vale, a valley, of ignorance."

"Still, I must to go Padua cementaire," Mazal said, with a stubborn look on her face. "I large passion desire to see, pray, holy man Rabbi Moses."

"Remember Rambam. His name was Rabbi Moses too. No go to dead."

She kept shaking her head. "Still, I go."

Now I shook my head. "Mazal, I think you're using here a conundrum."

At once she clapped her hands to her ears and said:

"Please! Not nice" — she pronounced it niece, like the French city on the Riviera — "to say about sex so public. In front moi and rav. And I almost ultra-Orthodox!"

"But you misunderstand what conundrum is." I said, containing my laughter. "A conundrum is a difficult, speculative question. Not what you think it is, which I won't pronounce here before you and Roni."

Now, poor girl, her cheeks turned red. First like a tomato, then aubergine. I thought the south Indian coloration would remain there forever.

"Oh, pardon moi. I regret. Excuse moi. I am so apologize. Please. Frogive moi."

"Is all right, cher Mazal," I said.

"So what is condrum I use?"

"To reconcile magic and superstition with synagogue politics."

I figured she might not know what reconcile meant. So I added, "It's probably *reconciliation*, in French."

She may not have known it in French either, for she did not react. She just repeated:

"I go Padua. Must," and pointed to her heart, as if to say that is the directive she is following. Obeying passion and desire. Not small like her English. But large like her penchant for prayer.

After gazing at her heart, her two not small hearts, I looked for a moment at Roni. But the rabbi did not say a word. Perhaps he sided with her. Perhaps he even regretted inviting me.

"But don't you realize you'll be consorting with the dead?" I couldn't help crying out.

I admit. I screwed up my hidden advantage. I couldn't button my lip.

"The prophet Samuel railed out against King Saul for consulting the Witch of Endor, trying to bring up a dead person."

Were Mazal older maybe I wouldn't have criticized a person I had just met. But since I considered her a kid I felt I could let my impulse fly sans restraints.

"Not witches," she insisted. "Not bring up dead. Tsk, tsk, tsk. No consort with morte, forbid of God! I want just to ...." and Mazal stopped when she saw me looking at the rabbi.

Still Roni said nothing. I was certain that he too would protest. Suddenly, Mazal folded her arms on her chest and began speaking in a louder tone. Her facial innocence vanished. She looked straight at me. I must have gone too far, gone beyond her ability to control herself. For she lashed out against me, saying:

"You know what? If you excuse moi, you, as they declaim in USA, full of bad linen." Then her face turned crimson again.

"I don't understand." I checked my shirt. Maybe she meant I had stained my shirt, which was cotton, not linen. "What do you mean by bad linen?"

"You Americain? And no comprend sleng?"

"Not this expression."

"On one arm you seem like nice," again said like niece, "Americain. On other arm you downput moi with your words. So I repeteat, in synonym words. Please excuse moi French, but I thinking all you say is pillowcase de bull. Pardon. Better say, how go expression, you full bull pillowcase."

I still didn't get it. I tried translating her Frenglish into American, stitching bad linen and bull pillowcase and — Oh, my God, I hit upon it — coming up with sheet.

Of course, no one else noticed this misplaced malapropism by Miss Paris, and, by now, I had learned to sublimate my risibility.

I'm surrounded by the Middle Ages, I thought. Me with Maimonides. Mazal with ibn Ezra. Mo and the mute woman I call Mu until I get to know her name, seemingly wrapped in a cloak of medievality. And of course, Mod, Leone da Modena, okay, late medieval on the cusp of modernity, whom I haven't forgotten.

Hey, there's a book title with all those *M's: Me, Mo, Mu, Ma & Mod.*

For a moment there was silence.

Then Roni said, with a little smile — had he caught all this?

Curt Leviant

— "Time to eat some more."

The rabbi rose to bring the next course. I looked back to Mazal. With a napkin she was dabbing at her perspiring brow. A bit of the mascara had run under her lashes, giving her the appearance of a black eye. She fanned herself, then rose and went to the window, evidently familiar enough with the apartment to know how to open it by pulling a latch and rotating a handle.

"I help rabbi," she said and went straight to the kitchen.

Umberto, sitting next to me, rolled his eyes. "I'm with you," he said. "I think it's madness running to a dead rabbino for salvation."

"You know," I said. "I disdain her narrow mind but I like her spunk."

"Spunk. What is that?"

I explained and Umberto laughed. "She also seemed to know exactly where the kitchen was without asking."

"I noticed that too. But to the Padua cementaire she'll definitely need directions. Do you have a hunch what's bothering the girl?" I asked him.

"Not really," he said. "But in their Moroccan culture, I assume she is Moroccan, they are keen on rabbis' blessings and amulets and touching tombstones."

I told him that Ashkenazim are no less enthusiastic on that score: knocking on wood. The evil eye — *kinnahoreh* in Yiddish. Spitting three times to avoid bad luck. The Hasidim and even non-Hasidim who run to rebbes for blessings, babies and cures. I told him about the cult of worship at the cemetery in New York where the Lubavitcher Rebbe is buried and the thousands of Bratzlav Hasidim who stream to Uman, deep in Ukraine, to pray at the grave of their leader, Reb Nachman, who also promised salvation, blessings, and good fortune to anyone who visits his grave.

"There's no stopping it," he said with a shrug. "It's universal."

I looked at my watch. "What's she doing in there so long with him?"

Umberto smiled; he raised his dark eyebrows. "My exact thoughts. You know...this girl, she's not what she appears to be**."**

"Hmm," I said, not really knowing what he meant. "Maybe she has her eye on the eligible bachelor rabbi."

"Could be. But she's a very confused girl. Womanly. Religious. Semi-educated. Big eyes seemingly full of naivete. But sexy. Very. Notice the words she used three or four times. Passion. Desire. Sex and sexiness just flows out of her."

"Like sap from a maple tree," I added. "Effortlessly. You got it. That's the operative word. Sexy. But with a coating of religiosity."

"That's what makes for the confusion," Umberto said. "And the pull. The attraction."

"In pagan societies," I said, "that was always a potent combination. Religion and sex. Do you know the sonnets of John Donne? Even the Torah rails out against the pagan holy whore, *kedesha*, using the same root letters, *k, d, sh* for the word holy, *kadosh*."

"I know, but don't forget," Umberto said, "we had it among our own too. Remember the harp-playing, giant-killer who wrote many poems in passion praise of God, which we recite daily in our prayers? But yet, even before David became king, and certainly after, he desired, loved sex, had women and children all over the place, including a few shikses, and at least one married woman."

About ten or fifteen minutes had passed and Roni and Mazal had still not emerged with the next course. The professor and I contin-

Curt Leviant

ued our exchange silently. We looked toward the kitchen. I spread my hands in a questioning gesture; the professor shrugged. He tilted his head one way, then the other, hinting that the two seemed to know each other. I nodded, then brought my hands together. He understood. All this made me recall my sign language conversation last Shabbat with the attractive mute woman, Mu, who had the two differently colored eyes.

Then Roni and Mazal returned, pushing a little table on wheels, on which were plates laden with stewed chicken and vegetables. Mazal helped the rabbi serve. We sat and ate quietly, speaking only to praise the food. Umberto took a few deep breaths during the meal, sniffing deeply, apparently savoring the fine aroma of the dishes the rabbi had prepared. And Mazal, to praise the rabbi's fare, looked at him with a smile and said, "Rabbi is tres bon cookie. He maybe certainment study kitchening."

At one point in the meal when Mazal excused herself, probably to go to the bathroom, I took the opportunity to say:

"Seeing graves, although entrenched in Jewish folklore, is basically pagan. You heard me mention Rambam's opposition and Samuel and the Witch of Endor."

I thought the rabbi would be taken aback at my implicit criticism of his silence toward his guest's hoped-for mission. But then again, with Aden/Yemen as his heritage, he too was probably raised with a load of superstitions.

His measured tone surprised — and pleased me too.

"On principle, you are absolutely right," Roni said judiciously. "And you argue your point with precision and passion." At this now potent word Umberto and I exchanged a swift, secretive glance. "But it should be said, and I don't know if you can notice it, but Mazal is," and here the rabbi dropped his voice, "a troubled girl, seems to be torn with [I am sure he meant "between"] super-orthodoxy and freedom, if you know what I mean. Pulled in two different directions. As a writer I am sure you noticed this too... But go a little easy on her, okay? By the way, how do you know so much about Bible and folklore?"

"Like Seneca said, everything human interests me, especially Judaism, so I read a lot."

"So, then," the rabbi continued, "if she considers that encounter crucial for herself or her community, who am I either to say don't or counsel her away from this quest?"

As the rabbi spoke I saw the wisdom of his words. I realized I was being as ornery in my own way as Mazal was in hers. Perhaps even a bit fanatical. One can be fanatical about anti-fanaticism too. Still, Judaism hitched to paganism has always annoyed me. And superstition too. In any case, the rabbi's approach seemed to be that Mazal wasn't violating any basic laws of Judaism.

"If the aura of the dead rabbi's spirit would give her and her community back home some psychological strength or inspiration — all the better. Her visit to the Padua cemetery will very likely do her a lot of good."

Of course neither he nor I could tell how prescient his words would be.

At that point I had not yet known what I would learn later: Rabbi Moses had indeed been buried in the old Jewish cemetery in Padua, but because of disturbances there over the centuries no one knows the precise spot of the Master of Padua's grave site.

Still, I said, "And she may not even find his grave."

"That's true. In these centuries-old Italian cemeteries sometimes it's hard to find a specific grave. For some reason the ones in our cemetery on the Lido are very well preserved. But, as I said,

I think even the search will be psychologically beneficial, you'll see."

"What will you'll see?" Mazal asked, suddenly appearing. The way the question was framed, in a tone so amicable and flirtatious, also showed a familiarity with the rabbi. With my love of the outré, I could almost hear the word "honey" at the end of her question.

And the rabbi answered at once. "You'll see that in time salvation and joy will come to the people of Israel. That is God's promise to us."

"Amen," she said, eyes closed, and tilting her head up piously in the Moroccan manner.

We continued eating. Now the silence was so massive and dense in this high-ceilinged room it took on the shape of the room, like a balloon filling with air. Each knock of a fork on porcelain resounded. I looked at Mazal's face and noticed, for the first time, her well-shaped lips, the hint of a pout adding allure. With every breath the bare flesh visible in her open blouse rose and fell. And then she interrupted the stillness with:

"I praying, hoping, maybe Rabbi Moses coming to me in dream assist moi. I try all kind dormir positions pour aider dreams."

Which at once prompted me to imagine various impious positions.

Again all eyes were on Mazal.

"Do you dream better on side, back, front?" she continued, looking at each of us. Now for the first time, as she spoke, she kept running her hand through her hair, brushing it back, pulling it forward and pushing it back again. "Pour example, I usual dorm on moi derriere, sometime on moi belly..." She gave "belly" a French twist, giving it Gallic panache by accenting the final "ly." "But I no have no dreams in disposition, for squeezed are my grand tetons, tres manhandled from weight of moi."

I looked over to the rabbi to see his reaction to this personal, very sensual confession. Thought he would be embarrassed, look off into the distance, hoping this would soon end. But Roni did not blanch, did not look uncomfortable. Au contraire, he seemed rather interested. At one point he opened his mouth as if to interject a comment, then apparently changed his mind.

Umberto, who hadn't been very talkative, said:

"I compromise. I go to sleep on my back and wake up on my side, but can't dream in any position."

"*E tu?*" Mazal turned to me.

"I cannot tell. It is totally dark in my room when I fall asleep."

"Come," she said. "You must to be say laugh."

"*Mais non.* I'm not saying joke. I never telling joke. And when I upwake it is also so dark I cannot see dreams on the screen of moi mind."

Mazal waved her right at me with a gesture that writers call "disparaging". (Have you ever seen this word used in any other context except with "remark" and "wave"?)

"So leave le luminaire on," was her quick riposte, chin down, a little smile on her lips.

Then she turned to the rabbi, her big dark eyes open wide. Did he note in that headlight beam a seemingly provocative glance?

Roni didn't hesitate; he didn't equivocate; didn't say, I don't answer personal questions. But he did put a rabbinic spin on his reply.

"Dreams come unbidden, as Joseph knew, although I have

recently read in a London *Times* science column that some people actually make preparations for certain dreams. But as for sleeping positions, I know there is an Ashkenazic edict, maybe it has the force of halakha, but I'm not an Ashkenazi so it doesn't apply to me — that a man should not sleep on his stomach for obvious reasons."

At that I feared Mazal would pipe up innocently: What are the obvious reasons?

"But me," Roni continued, "I sleep in all positions and dream in all of them."

"And let me question rabbi too." I said. "Is mamzell for similant raisins also prohibidden to dorm on her backside for obvious raisins?"

"You know," Roni replied, "that's a good question. I don't know. I never heard that aspect mentioned from a woman's point of view. So if you don't sleep on your belly, Mazal, because of discomfort, what position do you choose?"

"I start dorm on moi derriere, but in tumult of night, switch position, restless in excitation of yearny dreams...blankets cast dither and yong. And when dawn shatters and rooster pronounce matin, I full surprise find moiself at cockgrow."

To press my lips, to pinch my thigh, to swallow hard I had to. Lips buttoned. Obeying Bellow's edicts. Together very pressed. Mouth up-zipped.

Since I was the only native English speaker there, I don't think anyone else but me noticed that egregious, accidental, hilarious slip, that Freudian undergarment, so apropos for Mazal. But I thought, Ah, there's a key phrase, "restless in excitation of yearny dreams," that I would like to explore with her some other time. I love language, and I especially love it originally used. And, anyway, who else would she be when she wakes up if not herself — an inversion of her herself in her sex-starved cockgrow?

But Mazal wasn't done.

"And I find moiself," she continued, "up waking on my belly, the mattrois press moi grand tetons and a discomfortable, almost hurt, in moi tetons."

"Which one?" I teased.

She took a napkin to dab again at her moist brow.

"On that this side, le two," she pointed yither and dong, "so pressed, and take tres much time to way ago."

"You know what I've noticed," the rabbi with an upbeat tone, a bit loudly, no doubt to change the subject. A happy, childlike smile suffused Roni's face, as though he'd just made an amazing discovery. "Here, around the table, we have a diversity of ages, separated by decades."

"You," to Mazal, "in your mid-twenties."

"Me," pointing to himself, "I'm in my mid-thirties."

"You," to me, "in your early forties."

"And you," to Umberto, "early fifties."

"Actually, fifty-eight."

"Okay, and now," Roni said. "It's time to finish up the meal."

When it came to the Grace After Meals, with Mazal sitting opposite me as I recited the blessings thanking God for the food we had eaten, I had to close my eyes lest my intentions wander and I begin to bless other potent, delectable fruits. It was fortunate that Mazal had come in after we had washed our hands and had recited the blessing over the challah, for had she been there beside us in the kitchen as we were washing, instead of saying "*netilat* **ya**-*da-yim*" (taking hands, meaning; washing hands) I might very well have said in confusion, "*netilat* **sha**-*da-yim*" (taking breasts).

Both Umberto and Roni were sharp and perceptive. One called Mazal confused and sexy; the other called her troubled. The two pillars that rooted her were religion and sex. Right in line with Umberto's on-the-mark assessment of King David. Gauging the extent of Mazal's religiosity was problematic. She sent mixed signals. The way she dressed was one; her closed-eyes piety was the other. Given her declared "almost ultra-Orthodoxy", one would have expected her to be in the synagogue on Friday night (she wasn't there Sabbath morning either). And during the Grace After Meals she gazed down for a while at the little prayer booklet and then off into space. Again I thought of the beautiful Mu with one eye lavender blue and the other chartreuse green who also prayed desultorily and stared most of the time into a distance-less space. I thought I would see a fiery look in Mazal's big, clear brown, orange-flecked eyes, the intense ardor of someone who focused with high devotion and spiritual energy on the prayer. Outsiders sometimes call this the fanatic's gaze.

I kept wondering what wrong could Mazal have done that prompted her to take this long trip. What sin could she have committed? It was fun to speculate, but in this fun there was also a measure of agitas and irritation. Her thinking was probably this: If she saw the grave and bowed down or prostrated herself at the tombstone of the holy rabbi, some spiritual credit would accrue, like points, or merits, that she could bring back home to the Paris suburb and erase the blight hovering over her.

But I had a hunch it was more complicated than that. Let's see. What can my imagination come up with? First thing that struck you when you looked at this attractive, pleasantly ripe girl was that she radiated Eros. For her it was effortless, seemingly built into her genes. Some girls practice walking before a mirror. She didn't have to. She didn't have to do anything to accent her womanliness. When Mazal came into a room, as she did into the rabbi's dining room, one look at her in motion sufficed. With every step she took those two aforementioned bounties bobbed, but with a slightly different syncopation, in independent, offbeat rhythm.

So it had to be a man/woman problem back there in Paris. Then it hit me. I got it. The whole scene popped up like a stage set before me. Mazal said she was a teacher in the synagogue religious school. The rabbi there no doubt guided her. Spent a lot of time teaching her how and what to teach. Told her about ibn Ezra. Juices flowed. They do, willy-nilly, they do. Whether or not you are very almost ultra-Orthodox. So that was it. That's what happened.

The Paris rabbi's wife got wind of this, goes my scenario, and, at a public meeting, declared that some people were spending too much time with the rabbi, taking him away from his holy work, helping older people, the sick, the disabled. The wife did this all of a sudden, I speculated, at a community meeting regarding something else entirely. The accusation was not personal, but everybody knew who the wife was referring to. But other people had evidently stood up and, without mentioning names, asked the rabbi's wife what proof she had for this. This perhaps had caused the split, the tear, in her community. Some on this side; some on that. And by going to Padua to the grave site of Rabbi Moses, known for standing up for the wrongly accused and mediating public squabbles, Mazal could return and say to a group of equally superstitious people that the Master of Padua, Rabbi Moses, would defend her, even from the grave, which she had just visited.

He would defend her against patently false accusations, and the combination of the tombstone, cemetery, grave site, dead spirit, the well-known rabbi — all this would cast a pall of fear, dread, spirit-enervating terror over the Paris rabbi's wife and her supporters who would be scared to death that the dead Rabbi Moses would blight her days and haunt her nights.

All this was just supposition, to be sure. And, to be sure, I had a hunch it was also true.

A few days after our Friday night dinner I bumped into Umberto dei Rossi in front of the train station. He was on his way back home to Rome after spending a few days with colleagues at the University of Venice. He greeted me warmly and said, "The rabbi was perfectly right. Saying that that girl is torn between super Orthodoxy and freedom. I didn't want to be the first to say it. It's not my business. But to me she looks like a girl who could be very religious and then, with a snap, turn an about face. Remember? Passion desire?"

I nodded in agreement. "You think she knows the other meaning of those words?"

"Are you kidding? She invented them." Then Umberto added with a twinkle in his eyes, "You really were outraged the other night."

"I was."

"And you really let her have it."

"I did. I hate stupidity, especially religious stupidity. The denseness of it."

"But on a body like that."

"Yes. That's her saving grace."

"Did you see how she was teasing her hair as she spoke?"

the professor recalled. "She just constantly draws attention to herself. She has sex written all over her." Umberto stopped for a moment. "She even has," he continued, "a sex smell." He sniffed three times, quickly. "It came right across the table at me. It's like an invisible veil that surrounds hers."

I laughed. "More visible than invisible. So that's why you breathed in a few times during the meal. That's what you were sniffing. And I thought it was only the food."

Umberto smiled.

"But that still doesn't mitigate the superstitious nonsense she advocates," I added. "There are spectacles for nearsightedness and farsightedness. But no lens has yet been developed to correct shortsightedness."

5.5 Walk Alone

I woke up early; that is, I could not sleep. No matter which position. Was it Mazal, whom I will nickname, Ma, who had disturbed my sleep? Maybe yes, maybe no. My brain was too fuzzy to analyze it. It was actually still night when I got up, dressed, and began walking, pretending I was a tourist in the city. I didn't look at my watch but it was probably 4 am.

The full moon cast an eerie light on the deserted streets and empty squares.

As I moved forward the beneficent shadow of that grey bird with the white fuzz above its eyes that I had seen flying the other day guided me backward in time. I walked to the entrance of the Ghetto and recalled the Jews who had lived here hundreds of years ago. Once they left the Ghetto they had to return via this gate to their homes before nightfall, for at a certain hour the gates were locked and they could no longer enter. The entrance, now wide open of course, was right by a canal, at the edge of which, on the sidewalk, were chairs and tables from the local kosher restaurant. Around noontime diners would be eating their festive Shabbat lunch here. I walked up the narrow lane, past the little dairy restaurant on the right and the bakery on the left toward the Great Synagogue. In this square stood the old six-story apartment houses that dated back to Ghetto times when Jews lived here. These buildings, jokingly called 'skyscrapers,' are the highest residences in Venice, for most of the buildings, except for churches, are no more than three stories high. But the Jews of the sixteenth and seventeenth centuries were not allowed to build out — so they had to build up. But as the houses added on stories, the ceiling of each succeeding floor was a bit lower. By the time they reached the sixth floor the ceiling was barely two meters high.

Now I passed the square where to my left was the Jewish Old Age home, which had only six elderly residents, and the new hotel extension that had been added to it.

Of course at this hour no one was on the street. And even though I wore sneakers I still heard my lone footfalls, so quiet is Venice with no vehicular traffic. For the first time I noticed the two solitary trees in this concrete square. Here too were a few more, mostly unused, synagogues, some in the small Jewish Museum at the corner of the square. At the far left end, over a tiny bridge, is a small canal, an almost forgotten canal at the Ghetto's edge where you hardly ever saw a gondolier.

With the full moon shining on the Ghetto I imagined I was walking through a black and white film, my eyes the movie camera. I made my way, still alone, in the middle of the night, along Strada Nuova, the long street that leads you across little bridges to the great Piazza San Marco. In the water of these narrow canals one saw small boats covered with tarpaulin. But there were no gondolas here, for at night the gondolas rested in front of Piazza San Marco, where, in local parlance, the gondolas "sleep".

Now a pre-dawn gray light was rolling away the darkness. Morning was gliding in, silent as a gondola. I could no longer see the moon.

Then I passed laterally through one of the long buildings that framed a huge part of Piazza San Marco. I don't know if the tunnel-like passage was planned to enhance the drama of coming into the huge square. But the effect is certainly there — emerging from a short, dark walkway into the huge, open, light filled space — as is the pleasure of the view no matter how many times you enter the Piazza.

Not a soul was on the square. That enormous area, the largest square in Europe, was empty. And then, near the Bell Tower, I saw two men sweeping with long curved straw brooms. The chairs and tables of the outdoor cafes remained in place, thoroughly clean. And the pigeons walked about slowly in the center of square — not one of them in flight — pecking in vain at non-existent crumbs.

The Piazza seemed larger without people. And I liked it that way, for I was now its sole proprietor.

Suddenly, a slant of surprising light. The sun was coming up, lighting up the walls of the Doge's Palace. The shadows fleeing. I stood there in a trance. On a dawn like this, I wanted to, I wished I could stop time. I wished it would be five am forever on a cool, sunny, mid-summer day, with the rising sun painting rose the old buildings and making the windows glint with light. Some long puffs of clouds are scattered picturesquely on the azure sky. I look up for that bird whose shadow rode for a while above me, but it is not there. The only thing I see flying are clouds over the Adriatic Sea.

They seemingly do not move, the clouds, but yet if one looks away for a moment and then gazes up at the sky, the cloud pattern has changed. And the silence, that almost humming silence, is pervasive. The silence that is the trademark of Venezia. There is not even a dry leaf on the great square to rustle as the wind comes in from the sea, nor the cry of a hawk circling overhead.

I felt a spurt of joy seeing the full moon and the rising run within the space of an hour. Years ago, on a trip through Israel's

Negev desert, early one morning, during one enchanted moment, I saw the full moon setting in the West and the sun rising in the East. Then, to me, they were only beautiful celestial bodies.

Today, the moon and the sun had a different meaning for me. Now they were text and subtext; text and commentary. When I regarded the moon I thought of Mu, cool, silent, a bit distant, perhaps willfully, perhaps in reaction to the attitude of others; like the moon's, her light did not touch you. And when I looked at the sun, Ma came to mind, warm, close, filled with light. Like the sun you felt her presence on your skin. Her proximity was palpable. But let's not overdo parallels lest the comparisons crumble. Suffice to say that on this magic night-and-dawn walk I thought of both of them, the pretty woman who was mute and other pretty one who had lots to say.

Now I made my way back via the arched Rialto Bridge which spanned the Grand Canal. I crossed over and then turned right to pass the fish market, housed in a large elegant hall and the great produce market. Since the vaporettos had not yet begun to sail, the water of the Grand Canal was calm, reflecting the palazzos across the way. Side by side stood buildings from different eras, the years of their construction seen on their facade, as telling of age as rings on a tree trunk. Now in the light, the water reflected all the colors of the buildings, gray, white, buff, rose, mauve, in long watery colorful stripes. Although the palazzos were opposite me, I could bend down and touch their reflection. When I tried to pick up them up, the shimmering image vanished and I was left with a greenish liquid running through my fingers. That is the difference between the magic of Venice the eye can see and the reality the fingers can touch.

Before me was the Ca'Doro, the palace of gold, my favorite

of the great palazzos of Venice, the one I had purposely come to see. It stood on the other side of the Grand Canal glowing in the morning light, its facade glittering and waving slightly in the water. But only in the westering light of sunset is its full incandescence realized when a golden hue caresses its walls.

Now in the distance I heard the churning of the first vaporetto.

The night had ended, its silent magic gone; a new day had begun.

6 *Shabbat* Walk with the Silent Beauty

Later that morning — I didn't bother going to sleep — heart beating, I looked for Mu, the mute beauty, in the synagogue. Not there. (Neither was Mazal.) I left the Sabbath service early, hoping she would be at the Kiddush. The door to the courtyard was open. The women were setting the tables. But Mu was not there either. I walked out, strolled about in the Ghetto. Then I turned and — how my heart lifted, rose up; a cloud of rose scent enveloped me — suddenly saw her. Seeing me she smiled. And I was proud that she, so reticent with a smile, graced me with a smile. She opened her mouth as if to say something. Again my heart surged. She's going to speak. But she said nothing.

I walked toward her, said, "*Shabbat shalom*," and clasped her hand.

Mu nodded with eyes half closed.

Then, quite naturally, as if it were ordained, she put her right hand through my left and thus we walked, in the old-style European fashion as though we were a couple, away from the community building. But we had to stop several times, for although she could hear me, I had to turn to her to see what she was trying to tell me.

I wanted to look at my palm, but walking this way made it difficult, for I did not want her to note this. So I switched sides and she held my right hand with her left. This way I could glance quickly at my left palm without Mu seeing. I wanted to see if her magical word was still there. It was. I neglected to mention that once, only once, did I see the three-lettered *Shabbat* not in the cursive form on my palm, but in the square script as scribed in the Torah, שׁבת, as if she the scribe and I the parchment.

Another thing I noticed was just as mysterious. As we walked, I sensed an airy canopy over us, a diaphanous cupola whose outlines I could nevertheless see. It was as if a private bower of whipped fine gauze had been prepared for us, a bower no one could see. It was an imaginary chupah, wedding canopy. But who the groom, who the bride? I wondered if Mo and Mu, two strange figures in Venice, had ever met. But one thing I was sure of. If I would concoct a wedding, Rabbi Leone de Modena would officiate.

As we walked along the long main street, the Strada Nuova, she pointed out a little supermarket I'd never noticed. And then, taking a sudden left, she led me into a sestiere I hadn't been to before. Here the calles were wider and the buildings, of a reddish brown brick, seemed taller. What impressed me most was the lack of people. I felt I had stumbled onto an abandoned movie set. Behind the houses I saw a high steeple of a church. I suggested that we explore it. But no matter how we circled the buildings, we weren't able to find a path that led to the church. And where were all the residents?

I asked Mu how long she had been in Venice.

She placed her right hand on her heart and then cupped her hand and made backward waving motions next to her ear, indicating time gone by.

When I asked where she had lived before coming to Venice, she made a circular motion with her forefinger: all over this region.

And your profession?

Her reply was a little semi-arc that suggested tomorrow, tomorrow.

I gathered it was too difficult to explain with sign language. But that tomorrow made me happy for, without my asking her, she was reconfirming our planned get together for tomorrow.

It was lovely walking with her, but a feeling of unease hovered within me. I kept wondering throughout the week why she had suddenly disappeared last *Shabbat* as we walked out on the street after the Kiddush and after she had written *Shabbat* on my left palm. At first I held back, but then decided to ask her. But she did not reply. She sort of shook her head slightly and pressed her lips as if to indicate she couldn't explain it. Not that she didn't want to — she just couldn't. Then her face brightened and that alone, as if the light on her face had a magic radiance, made me feel better.

"Tomorrow?" I said. "Sunday."

She nodded.

"By the gondola station at the edge of the Ghetto. Is four in the afternoon good? At that time there is no rush for gondolas."

She agreed and we continued walking.

With her at my side I felt like a high school kid dumbstruck with the joy of his first date with the girl of his dreams. But that's an exaggeration, for femaleness did not flow out of her; she lacked the vibes that women like Mazal send forth. Not that she was sexless. I don't think that's the right word. It might be but I want to avoid it. Maybe neuter is better. As you can see, I'm still trying to assess her femininity, a tame, properly dressed word for womanliness. But then what was the pull, for I did want to see this pretty woman again. And she didn't even have a voice. A woman's voice can always allure; it's like a stringed instrument that can change its pitch, tone, notes, personality.

Perhaps. Maybe. Could be that....

Curt Leviant

Then what was it that pulled me if she didn't have that animal magnetism? One that flowed from Mazal, one that sent a wordless message: come, come, come to me. Me.

Me. Me. Ma and Mu.

Well, the mute woman had one power Mazal didn't have. The ability to inscribe letters into my palm. Perhaps Mu had blind-sided me with that other-worldly touch, when she wrote *Shabbat* on my hand to inform me she observes the Sabbath and does not write on that day. Perhaps that word imprinted on my palm was the incantation that made me follow her. Sealed into those let-ters, like deep within a computer, were tiny invisible magnets that commanded me, like a golem controlled by his creator: look at me, pay attention to me. And so, despite her lack of overt sexiness, I saw in her womanly grace, charm, that drew me to her, to the mystery of her, to the enigma of Mu.

But I must admit that at the edge of my consciousness was Mazal, magnetizing me with her eyes and everything else on her. By no means could I extirpate Ma. Not that I wanted to. But just as I knew I could see my silent companion again, there was no way I could contact Mazal. Although I could ask Roni, I wouldn't, especially after criticizing her so much in his presence. On the other hand, I could use a ruse. I could tell the rabbi there were a few more points I had thought of to dissuade Mazal from going to the Padua cemetery. Nevertheless, I would not call him because deep down I suspected there might be something between them.

What can I do? Both the silent woman and Mazal pulled me. In different ways. Ma was flesh, more or less; Mu spirit, ditto. I know it's too simplistic, but I call it as I see it. There must be a hi-falutin philosophical term for this flesh/spirit antithesis.

There always is.

Maybe Dionysian, the lustful, erotic, sensual, wild, unbridled passion of the pleasure seeker, and its opposite, Apollonian, signifying beauty, poetry, music, grace, clarity, a rational, thoughtful approach to the world. Wait. Maybe I'm mixing it up with Napoleonian, who also had a thinking man's approach to the world. Or maybe Apollonian, the angel of the bottomless pit. That extra "y" makes all the difference. Truth is, the Greeks always did cast dust into my eyes. They got me D's in philosophy and lit crit courses, whereas I did much better in all the others, with an overall average of C plus.

But I tell you, when I looked at the French girl, at her vivant, yearning eyes and the open collar of her low-cut blouse with the top of her breasts rising, a surge of heat pulsed in me; inchoate thoughts surged like a locomotive gathering speed.

I too, my motive was loco.

Or as they say in French — *fou*.

Perhaps it was Mazal's overt erotic pull that diminished the mute beauty and made her appear sexless in my eyes. A pie has only 360 degrees, and if Mazal takes up 333 of them, how much is left for Mu, the silent woman with the unforgettable eyes?

Ma I saw right into. Each time she mentioned God I saw Eros. She didn't know it but I did; religion for her was a protective cloth, a kind of aerie condom for her sexual nature. Her passion. Her desire. If she could have seduced Rabbi Roni — and maybe she did — she could have killed two stirds with one bone.

Didn't spark the same reaction, however, Mu with the oval face, one eye lavender, the other chartreuse. My insides didn't hum when I thought of her or looked at her. I didn't dream of her as I did about Mazal. For me she wasn't magnetic or a locus of desire. Her I wanted to hold and stroke tenderly and awaken the woman sleeping within her. Tender is central here. It's not for nothing that with sex the slang verbs most often used are on the anvil: bang, pound, hammer, knock, nail.

And maybe her silence drew me too. It added to her appeal, that Venice stillness and her sadness too. One doesn't get attracted to someone because of a physical defect. But if a woman is pretty to begin with, whatever flaw she has adds to the aura of simpatico around her. Perhaps that's why Mu's lack of voice fascinated me, drew me. As did her unusual way of walking, with its slightly off-rhythm, wooden gait.

Despite her nicely shaped body, it didn't assert itself. About Mazal everything asserted itself, even the words she uttered and the way she uttered them, with her lips moving as if she were kissing or blowing a kiss. But my mental embrace of the silent woman was an ethereal one, all air.

And you know what? Maybe all these suppositions are off the mark, for the three basic "L"s, likes and lusts and loves, are much more complex than banal casting them into two opposing categories like Dionysian and Apollonian. They slip all over the place like an oiled hand massaging an oiled body.

Was I walking with the silent beauty just to be nice? Because I felt sorry that she sat all by herself in the big courtyard during the *Shabbat* Kiddush? To break the network of distance that had been created around her because she was mute of tongue? I did ask myself this and I did ponder my reaction to her. But I also answered and I said no. Mu had an allure and I was taken by that allure, to that allure.

How is it that some women, even girls, radiate a womanliness, a sexiness, while others are bland as tea, even though they're as pretty as can be? Is it planned? Will power? Or is it a natural gift? An effusion of hormones? Nor diet nor exercise will achieve it. Mazal had it in plenitude; she must have had a reserve stock of it hidden somewhere under a strap. Ma didn't even look as if she were trying. It just waved out of her. But, alas, the attractive mute woman didn't have it. Yet she possessed something deeper than overt sexiness, something more profound, mysterious: a grace, a harmony, even if in that harmony lacked a note or two. For instance, the way she moved, as if she had learned to walk rather late in life; or her inability to smile at length, even if it were a pose, but that in itself added to her enigmatic allure.

Mu led me to a little courtyard that had lots of little calles leading away from it. She said goodbye and I turned to go. She went into one of those narrow lanes never lit by sunlight, those cobbled streets no more than two arms' length wide that carry the sounds of talking and the clackety clack of footfalls to the highest story.

And tomorrow afternoon a gondola ride with her.

Tomorrow I will ask Mu to write her name.

And I will finally learn the name of the silent woman with the two differently colored eyes.

7   On a Park Bench Near the Biennale

Via Garibaldi is unique. I've said it's my favorite Venetian street. In a city compressed as a pocket dictionary, with so many calles, narrow streets, and tiny dead-end alleys, it's a joy to walk on a street so wide that were it a canal an aircraft carrier could easily sail through it.

There, the very next day, Sunday at 11, the same day I was supposed to take Mu for a gondola ride at 4 in the afternoon, I bumped into Mazal, my buxom nemesis from that Friday night dinner at the rabbi's house. There she sat, on a bench, at the edge of the park near the Biennale, which abutted Via degli Schiavone, the waterside promenade that led to St. Marks Square.

Ma sat there staring out into space. Today she wore a short blue paisley skirt and a sleeveless light blue cotton t-shirt, cut so low it focused on her cleavage even more than on that recent Friday night when I first met her. Her crossed legs showed off her tan thighs; she made no effort to pull down the edge of her skirt. As she breathed the upper part of her breasts floated up and down like separate living creatures. The t-shirt and skirt sent out a message: interpret me, both sang out — and on key too. And what's more, today Ma wasn't so heavily made up around the eyes, which made her look even more attractive.

"Shalom," I said, "what a lovely surprise."

She frowned, probably remembering our contretemps.

"It was so nice meeting you the other night. Even though I disagreed with you, I must admit you had fascinating things to say. You have lots of spunk. Don't worry, that's a compliment, event though it rhymes with skunk. Spunk is a good word, meaning verve, energy, courage, with a dash of charm."

Still silent, but the frown vanished and a hint of a smile appeared.

"And with such a mellifluous voice too. Soon as I heard your melodic voice at the door when you came in to the rabbi's apartment I knew you'd be attractive. I can tell from a girl's voice what she looks like and I knew at once you'd be pretty, and I was right. And sexy too."

Now Mazal looked up at me full face, with a happy smile.

"Merci pour you nice words." Again she pronounced it like the French city, Niece.

"So what are you doing here?"

"Thinking to what to doing next." She pressed her index finger to her right cheek, assuming a cogitative pose. For the first time I noticed a little dimple on the other cheek.

"I a small lost. Grand problematique. Family I stay with, now no room. Daughter came back surprise, from visit London..."

There goes my wild thought that she'd secretly been staying at the rabbi's apartment.

"And I jogging out of euro and no place to dormir and no go yet to Padua. And in three day, plane ticket retour home."

Uh-oh, I thought. Next comes a request for funds, formulated in the traditional: Can you lend me money? And I'll pay you back soon as I get home, I swear.

"I'm so sorry to hear that, Mazal."

She brightened; a little flush of color waved through her cheeks. "You remember moi name?" And gave me a big smile. Now both dimples appeared which gave her face a child-like look.

She doesn't carry a grudge, I thought. Not one ounce of rancor for my relentless attack on her superstitious beliefs.

"Of course, Mazal. How could I forget?"

Again she smiled. This time her eyes had a naughty twinkle. "You speechify longlishly in rabbi apartment. And now, with spunk." She pronounced it "spoonk".

"You're right." A thought runs through my mind. Should I tell her? Yeah, why not? "Do you know, I've been thinking of you. I even dreamed of you?"

And at once she said:

"Verite?" she said in French. "Is non beliefable! And I have dream of you."

Wow! An exchange of dreams. An exchange of dreams must mean something. Even if she's pretending. No. She isn't sophisticated enough to be sly. Wait! Even if she didn't dream about me, the fact that she quickly said she did makes it as good as if she really did. Maybe even better. Not maybe, *surely* better. And then I began to ponder. I do ponder and think sometimes, even though I don't consider myself an intellectual. Which is better for the ego? runs through my mind. If she really dreamt about me, or if she didn't but said it to be nice, to show a bit of affection. Now that I thought of it, letting me believe that she dreamt of me was a notch more intimate, something akin to if we were alone she would look straight at me, purse her lips, and make a kissing motion with her lips.

"What you dream of moi?" Mazal asked.

In response to her flirtatious tone, I told her my dream. We ride on a vaporetto around Venice, take an elevator to the top of the Bell Tower on Piazza San Marco, and board a train for a trip outside of Venice. But I didn't tell her that in one scene we're back in the rabbi's apartment. Rabbi Roni had come out of the kitchen while she remained there, and I went in for a glass of water. And in the strange geography and distortion of dreams, I see her first through the glass and then in the glass and I swallow her along with the water. Then she stands before me, entirely wet, with every contour of her shapely body outlined.

For some reason, during the recitation of my dream, in another part of my brain, I re-see that semi-colon that had risen from my Siddur in the synagogue a week earlier floating across my line of vision. But now, to make itself readily visible, it is bright red, that tiny period, that modest comma; that assertive, colorful semi-colon.

And there was another dream I didn't tell her about. Boy, she kept me busy that night. I dreamt that I had brought Mazal into my apartment. I didn't realize mother is sleeping, but I can't tell if it's her mother or mine. I hide Mazal in a closet. Then I get into bed with her and mother walks in and takes it quite naturally, as if Mazal were my wife. In the dream Mazal is not simplistic or primitive. She's slimmer and not as flirtatious or provocative as in real life.

After that beneficent dream a line came to me: Dreams contradict intuition. I like three-word sentences, noun verb noun, especially if they have a proverbial ring and contain compressed wisdom, like a folk saying. That said, I still don't know what those words mean.

Throughout my narration, Mazal was smiling.

"Elevator, going up up up, is always *siman tov* in dreams."

Again favorable alignment of stars, again astrology, but this time I wasn't going to argue with her. I had the buttoned-lip syndrome down pat. This innocently erotic interpretation I rather liked.

"So you know meaning of dreams?" I said.

"Dreams tres important. Sometimes say what to be happen. Tell life.... I Witch of Endor, tres goodly in dreams." Then she laughed and added, "You travel with me muchly. On water. From side. In air. Up and down."

"Okay," I said, catching that clever Witch of Endor dig. "Now what's your dream of me?"

She lowered her head shyly for a moment. "You visit me in Paris school and clocking me teach. After class I fly, you fly next to moi, to Venezia."

A flying dream, I thought. Another bit of Eros. Dream experts always put a sexual interpretation on flying dreams.

"That's a wonderful dream. Flying dream, Freud said, is double *siman tov*."

Mazal cocked her head to gauge if I was poking fun or really meant what I said. Surely she remembered my tirade against belief in astrology. Then she checked her watch.

"Biennale door open in ten minute and I go."

"But doesn't it cost a lot of money? I wanted to go too, but I refuse to pay fifteen euros to see art. I thought you jogging out of money."

"You right. After I buy billet I jog out. But a person must to having fun, non?"

Could I say, No? So of course I said, "Yes."

Her interest in art astonished me. Given the religiously primitive front she had presented at the rabbi's house the other night, I was sure she would have no interest in art, akin to most people in the ultra-Orthodox circles, who consider art a form of idol worship.

"You looking laughy at me. Something not right? I contra-dictioning moiself? I know. No money, but fifteen euro pour museum."

"No, it's not that. I'm thinking of what you said in the rabbi's house the other night. About visiting a grave site."

I wanted to stop. I should have stopped. Now that the conversation was going so smoothly, so boy and girly on a frictionless path, why did I repeat myself and say:

"It's sort of strange, isn't it? In today's world, in modern times, consorting with the dead? Especially since Maimonides said No. Yes, rather strange."

And then I pulled the emergency brake that buttoned my lip.

"Okay. Sorry, Mazal. Pardon. Excuse moi. No more of this."

But today Mazal was not combative, as witness:

"I thinked goodly fun today tween I and you. No seriose argutation. But you smart man, you know all us human people, we do strange. And you, you no do strange?"

"Yes, Mazal. You are very wise." And I meant what I said. I took both her hands. "You are right, Mazal." And I pressed her fingers. "We human people, yes, we do strange. And now listen." My dream of her floated back to me. "Now *I* am going to do strange."

Ever since that mute woman with the two differently-colored eyes wrote *Shabbat* on my left palm I tended to keep that hand closed. But now as I released Mazal's hands I unwittingly spread open my own.

"That? *That* what is?" Mazal cried out.

And I realized that she was the first outsider to see that word imprinted on my palm שבת .

"Oh," I said, while wondering what to say to not sound absurd. Then it dawned on me to sing out: "That's a reminder to me to keep the *Shabbat*."

By now she had seized my hand and was inspecting the word.

"That is tres nice." Again she pronounced the word like the Riviera resort city. "So non usual. Usual, people inscript words in heart."

"Very true," I said.

"Who is persona what inscripted you? An artiste de tootoo?"

"But you know tattoos are proscripted by Torah," I said.

"Certainment I knowing."

"So how could I have made tattoo?"

French style, she shrugged and stuck out her lower lip.

"Possible you can descript inscript from hand?"

"Non non. Non wish to. I wake up one day and it was there. Message..." I pronounced it messahge to give it a French flavor, "....from divine."

"In realitay? So fortunate you to having massage of angel. To having *Shabbat* inscripted in hand. To you now easy pour recall *Shabbat*."

I nodded shyly.

"I wish angel give moi massage....Mazal, go to Padua!"

"Maybe surely time will come when moi give you fine massage." And as I spoke, I watched carefully for her reaction to that suggestive word. But it passed her by.

"Is miracleuse. And I impressionistic and joyeuse that smart man like you is *shomer Shabbat*, that you watch with care to follow *Shabbat* customs."

Again Mazal took my hand and looked at my palm.

"*Borukh ha-shem*," she said with passion, closing her eyes like a nun and raising her eyes skyward. "Thanking Dieu pour miracleuse petite and grande."

And with that "Blessed be God" in Hebrew, Ma ran her thumb ever so smoothly and lightly over the three letters, perhaps hoping that some of the magic would rub off on her. Mazal's touch sent a tingle through me that radiated out from the locus of the letters through every nerve of my body.

Finishing me off.

And more:

With that touch of hers, her finger rubbing my palm, I saw Leone da Modena and my entire Venice writing project receding, getting even smaller. But yet, but still, but nevertheless still still there. For a while I had thought that perhaps the attractive Mu would somehow be woven into the Modena story. But that too had faded. The real story, the real fiction, was developing under my nose here in Venice. Yes, she would be woven, but not into Modena. And Mazal, she would be woven too. Into me.

Truth is the greatest fiction.

Yes, I was looking at Modena from the far end of a telescope, but I didn't want to drop him altogether for this rabbi of many professions was so fascinating. Mod kept slipping away; yet when I thought of him, he zoomed back at me.... I was torn in two directions, trying to hold on to both. In short, I had not kissed him a definitive goodbye. And I wasn't forgetting Mo either, that strange bearded man with the slight Spanish accent, the first person I had encountered in the Ghetto. In other words, all parts of the title were dancing before me.

Then Mazal remembered. "What do you strange?"

"I'll tell you."

And as I spoke I put both my hands on the upper part of Mazal's arms. And as I spoke I moved my hands up and down a bit, gently stroking the flesh, much as she had tingled me when she rubbed, stroked, the palm of my left hand, as she ran her fingers over each of the three Hebrew letters, vivifying the dormant current in them. And as I spoke I noted a little shudder of pleasure running through her, my touch touching her. And then a soft, ecstatic sigh of joy, a little groan of pleasure. And as I spoke I asked her if she felt in her right arm the glow of the Hebrew letters.

She thought a moment and said, "Oui, moi arm feel warm.... Tres warm. Mmm, a goodly feel warm....And so tell, tell what do you strange?"

"Okay, here is what I do strange. You say you have no money. You say you have no place to sleep." And as I spoke I looked straight into her big, sparkling eyes, which had that unusual hue, dark brown dotted with tiny little orange flecks — eyes that looked much older than her twenty-four or twenty-five years.

"And so, since I have an apartment given to me by a foundation at no cost to me, call it a stipendium..."

"Oh! Foundation. You scientist?"

"No. Fictionist. Writer. Histoire. Livres. Roman."

"I am tres impressionistic. Ooh, livres! Roman! Moi heart so affection pour romanians."

I looked at her chest. "You have great big heart, Mazal. Un tres grand coeur."

"So you knowing French tres bien," she said. "And I thinked you no overstand francais."

"Very small overstand."

"So how you knowing kilometer long words *abomination* and *reconciliation*?"

"You remembered those words? Tu est amazing, cher Mazal! But you see, those big words are easy for me because most kilometer words are the same in French and English. It's the little French words that are difficult. Now back to what I do strange. Listen. Till you have to fly home and even longer, as long as you like, I am inviting you to stay with me in my apartment."

Mazal did not shake her head in astonishment; she did not say, with prissy modesty, No, no, thank you. So niece of you, but I no can do that.

She did say, "I telling merci merci, from top of moi heart, but I wish you must to recall je suis, I am Jewish girl."

"How could I forget that, Mazal? Do you think I think you are Neapolitan or Nepalese, Kazakhstanian or Congolese? Your Jewish girlness," at which I glanced with tres admiration, "bubbles bursts and bulges out of you."

Mazal thought this a compliment, so again she said, "Merci merci. Since I religious Jewish girl I must to be care of full and must to be wary wary in relationboat with boys, for as I say last clock I saw you, I almost ultra-Orthodox, as modest as they come."

That last phrase, so perfect in pitch for American English, and so out of harmony with her picturesque Frenglish, astounded me.

My eyes took in Ma's ultra-modest breasts and modern Orthodox thighs. Again I placed my hands on her upper arms and stroked them slightly.

"Not to worry. I am almost ultra-heterodox and I too am modest when I come."

"So please to recall that I not like lose modern girls. At snoop of digits" — and here she snapped her fingers — " them dropsy le pantsies to make ficky-focky."

Her choice of words astonished me, but I guess it's always easier to use forbidden words when you're talking a foreign language.

"You think I have no power of recollect, molestingly modest Mazal? No memory? Do you think, cherie, I do not recall Friday night dinner at rabbi Roni's house where together we imbibe wine? Chant Kiddush? In no way did I ever recall that you are a Christian concubine, a Muslim maiden or a gentile gypsy. But let us not drive ourselves debauchingly demented with absurdist terminology like modern Orthodox, ultra-Orthodox, modern loose, ultra-modest. Or, worst of all, ultra-heterodox. These religio-political movements mean nothing to me. How can I forget that you are a Jewish girl, Mazal, with your beautiful stunning gold-flecked Jewish eyes and that voluptuous Jewish Parisian French North African Moroccan body?"

That these voluptuary, concupiscent, Columbus-inspired adventurous New York Jewish hands would love to explore, for I too, like Mazal, am restless in excitation of yearny dreams.

"Very tres merci," she said. "I think you say niece romanian things to moi. And again you speechify longishly like rabbi in *Shabbat* sermon, where Jews in synagogue, all fall down asleep and no one overstands, because you English vocabular behind moi comprendition."

And then I added, "And you know of course that I am, je suis, Jewish boy."

"Certainment. So I like you to —"

"And I like you too," I interjected.

"No, I wish telling, I teach ebreu and Judaismic objects in religion school in Paris in moi synagogue."

"Good. Goodly."

"So *s'il vous plait*, please to respect this when I dormir with you."

I unclasped my right hand from her upper arm and raised it.

"It is within my learning tradition, from my beloved mama and papa, to respect my elders and suspect my younger intellectuals."

"Merci pour you for this respectfulness. I tres admirable you for this." And then, after a pause, Mazal added, "Will I must to dormir in solitaire bed?"

And in my thoughts I write: she asked hopefully.

"You will dormir either on bed and I on sofa. Or you on sofa and me on bed. Your choice. That is for first night only. For second night, either both of us on sofa or both on bed, but bed is more comfortable. Or, third choice, all of us under bed."

She laughed right away, but I don't know if it was for the second night or the third choice.

"You full of funny. You make all girls laughy."

"That sentence is correct. Even without the laughy."

As I spoke to Mazal there were other things I recalled. I did not forget the low cut t-shirt she was now wearing that showed the entire range of the Grand Teton mountain range, nor the low-cut blouse she wore that Friday night to the rabbi's dinner, or how she came late and right away opened the window, saying how hot it was and fanning her face with her hand, or how she disappeared into the kitchen with Roni for ten or fifteen minutes while Umberto and I waited for the next course. It was obvious that this was not the first time she had come to the rabbi's house.

And then I recalled another part of my dream that I had forgotten. So I told Mazal that in my dream of her she said she was a midwife.

"Midwife? Is midwife middle wife? Like man have three wifes and second is midwife? Or is midwife like middleman only feminile?"

"No. A midwife helps a woman deliver a baby. You know, when stork comes with baby, midwife helps give it to mama."

"And in your dream, like this I do?"

"Not really. Better. In my dream you said something very profound. You said you were a midwife of thoughts. That is, you help explain other people's thinking."

"Means you thinking of me intelligent."

"Yes. Yes, Mazal. That's one way of looking at it."

But there was also another way: in my dream I was perhaps hoping she would think clearly and not superstitiously, like so many of the North African Jews, fixated on wonder-working dead rabbis or praying to them to intercede with the living.

Again came that fool pushing me. An expression that needs explication. Whenever I did something dumb as a youngster, my mother would use the Yiddish expression, *der nar shtupt dikh*; literally, the fool is pushing you. Which meant that an irresistible force to do something foolish has come over someone and he can't stop himself from doing it. Only after the damage is done does he realize his dumb deed.

Luckily, I stopped myself from discussing the other way of looking at it.

"You know," Mazal said, with a little smile on her lips. Her big brown eyes with the golden little flecks there was a twinkle in them. "You mean but niece."

"You mean I'm nice and mean. But I mean to be niece."

"And you speechify with grand passion, though I small agree."

"That's me. Full of passion."

"You really mean invitation?" She pronounced the last word in French.

Wait a minute! Was she punning with the word "mean"?

"Of course I mean. Because I'm niece not mean."

"Bon. Merci. I come tomorrow in post meridian."

"Goodly."

"But prima, you must to give me something."

Oh no! Again money? I have to pay *her* for giving her free accommodation? Hold it! Bite your lip. Rein in the sarcasm. But maybe she didn't mean that and I would embarrass her by pulling out my wallet.

Maybe the something she wanted was a hug. But I better ask her first.

"What?"

She smiled. Again that naughty twinkle in her eye. With that look she seemed to have the upper hand.

"You address."

I wrote in a piece of paper and told her the calle was not far from the synagogue.

When she left, I don't know why, but my original subject, Rabbi Leone da Modena, floated into my ken, as if to say: You may have forgotten about me, but I haven't forgotten about you. Gamblers like me are trained to have sharp memories.

Long and sharp!

I said to myself: the next time I meet Mazal, I'm going to tell her: You look terrific. A warm womanliness shines forth from you, creating a warmth in me. You have a radiant sexiness. It is almost palpable.

But, then again, she might not know what palpable means, so I'll say:

One can almost touch it. In fact, if one takes a deep breath, even thinking of you, picturing your image, the scent of you, your sexiness, as if scent from a rose, it just floats out of you.

And I imagined Mazal's response, in her broken Frenglish:

What you say make moi so happy. So beautiful words. I felt like moi go backing in time and heard so similarious words to what moi been told by moi first friendboy, who study to be rabbinatical. You words they make a slow fire burn singeing in moi heart.

8   Walk and Gondola Ride with Mu

Precisely at 4 pm we both arrived, from different directions, at the appointed spot near the gondolier's station. Mu looked as pretty as usual; and more, her cheeks had a roseate glow. Her light beige cardigan, I think it was cashmere, over a short-sleeved, white blouse, and light brown slacks added to her appeal. Although it was warm, she had probably assumed it would be chilly during the gondola ride and hence the sweater. Hanging from her shoulder on a long thin strap was a little bright green alligator skin pocketbook. That bag was a beautiful touch, in the shade of green you see when the sun shines through a young maple leaf early in April, the shade of transparent bright chartreuse you see when you looked into one of her eyes.

"Shalom, so nice to see you, especially on a day that's not *Shabbat*." No more small talk, I decided. Let's get to the core. "Now it's time. I told you my name that day in the courtyard, but I —"

She interrupted me with a raised finger. She knew exactly what I was going to say and was telling me to wait.

Into her little pocketbook she went and took out a three-by-five inch paper pad and a pen. I looked, enthralled, at her long, elegant fingers as she wrote in English, "I have a little device that looks like a cell phone but it's like a typewriter. And that's how we will be able to talk."

"Wonderful," I said.

She took it out, flipped open the lid, typed with one finger, then showed me the screen.

"Gila."

I held both her shoulders.

"I'm so happy to finally know your name. You see, I'm so excited I even split an infinitive. Do you know what it means?"

She wrote: "Yes. When you put a word between 'to' and the verb."

I laughed. "No no. I meant, do you know what your name means?"

"Of course," she wrote. "Joy. Happiness."

"And it fits right in with you," I said, stretching truth a bit, for tristesse seemed etched into her. Maybe her wise and insightful parents had given her this name as a countervailing force, a kind of magical appellation, against the nature they knew, sensed, would possess her.

Now that I knew her name she seemed more beautiful than ever. Having a name made her more complete, a kind of final touch to her three-dimensionality. Until now, I confess, unable to think of her by name, I had given her a nickname, Mu (pronounced "moo"), for mute, just as I had shortened Mazal to Ma.

Soon as I thought of Mu and Ma, at once the other two protagonists of my title appeared before me: the bearded Mo, whom I met when I first entered the Ghetto; and the subject of my supposed short or long fiction in Venice, that rabbi of many professions, that fascinating Venetian figure, Rabbi Leone da Modena, whom I call Mod. Then, of course, to round it out, there's Me.

With Gila I could now reprise all my memories of her and give her face a name. For a name humanizes, gives color to gray; flesh and soul to a creature. Only after Adam named all the animals did they become whole. And a newborn baby becomes a person when it gets a name. No wonder totalitarian regimes gave numbers to prisoners and took away their names. Just looking at Gila's sad and pretty face that now possessed a name made me happy, gave me *gila*, gave me joy.

Gila. Gila. Gila.

"So you know Hebrew," I said. But that was a ridiculous remark. Of course she knew Hebrew. She had written *Shabbat* into my palm.

"*Ken*," she wrote. The Hebrew word for yes.

"But your little pad, it's not...." I hesitated. "It's not a phone."

"No, not a phone," she wrote, "for I have no use for that. But with this little gadget...I call it my little pad..." She stopped typing for a moment, looked at me with a smile in her eyes, "I can tell people what I'm thinking."

Then she closed her pad and indicated with index finger and hand, Come, let's go,

Gila held me by the arm, as usual, and we strolled through the well-traveled lanes that led to Piazza San Marco. I had walked this route before, knew almost all the shops and bridges — but somehow, while walking with Gila, I saw them through new eyes, one lavender, the other chartreuse.

At one point she stopped and took my right hand with her left. Then she did something unusual. She put each of her fingers on each of mine, pinkie on pinkie, thumb on thumb, middle finger on middle finger, ring and index finger too. It reminded me of the scene in the Bible where the prophet Elisha, to revive the seemingly dead son of the woman who had provided him with room and food, lies on the boy, chest to chest, face to face, hands on hands. And Gila, with each finger, while warm buzzes went

Curt Leviant

through me, Gila spread open my palm and looked at it.

Would she now inscribe on my right hand too the word *Shabbat*, to enhance the spell she had cast over me? To strengthen it? Double it? For in nature balance is essential. What is done for one side of the body, in classical exercises, is done for the other. For that is the path to health. And the more I thought of it, the more I realized that that is what should be done. I should have those three Hebrew letters, *shin, bet, tav*, that spell *Shabbat* inscribed in my right palm too. But I would not ask her to do this. Under no circumstances would I, or should I, do this. There are certain gifts that cannot be requested.

As she held my hand and looked at my palm, for a moment I thought Gila was Mazal seeing my left palm for the first time and being amazed at the Hebrew word written on it.

"You do strange," I said, mimicking the tone and the word I had used with Mazal earlier in the day and falling naturally into her phrasing. "Why do you strange?"

Was Gila looking to see if her word was still there? Had she forgotten it was on my left hand and not the right? Or would she indeed now put that word on my right hand too, the hand that is symbolic for strength, the hand used as a potent image for God's power, His right hand? Save us—the age-old prayer states—with the might of Your right hand.

But Gila didn't answer me. She didn't take out her little pad and type a reply.

Then she took my left hand and inspected it too. She opened it, not in the same manner she had with my right hand, saw the *Shabbat*, and gave a slight nod, as if pleased. So that's it. She wanted to see if her word was still there and had apparently forgotten on which hand she had inscribed the word.

"It's still there, Gila, don't worry," I said, "still pulsing, still alive."

She lifted my hand and brought it closer to her face, still gazing at it. Seeing this, I thought she would lift my palm to her mouth and kiss it. But she did not. She gently lowered my hand, took my arm, and we continued our walk.

And maybe it was good she did not kiss my palm. The intensity of her lips on the words she had inscribed into my skin would have been too much for me. Like dark energy suffused with supernova.

"You do strange. But I like the way you do strange. You do strange like no one on the face of this earth do strange," I said, looking into Gila's eyes, first the one green chartreuse and then the other, blue lavender.

For a moment I was sucked into the deep arena of her eyes and I felt a touch of dizziness. The color of her eyes swirled around me like a compressed spectrum. But then I drew my head back, retreating, as if distancing myself from her.

Now she took out her little pad and, as I watched, slowly pecked at the keyboard. "You no speak grammatical but I like the way you speak no grammatical."

I laughed, pleased at her joke; the first time she had shown me her sense of humor. Now she smiled and I saw her teeth. Another first? Was this the first time I saw her full-fledged smile? Maybe not. I do not recall, for when I was with her I couldn't rely on my memory, because the pulses in her *Shabbat* bent my sensibilities, like gravity bends light.

Then I took both her hands and opened them the way she had opened mine. I wanted to see if perhaps she too had a Hebrew word inserted into one, or both, of her palms. But I saw nothing.

Curt Leviant

Gila knew what I was looking for. She shook her head, then wrote, "Only on yours."

Again three words.

Affirming that only on my hand had she inscribed that Hebrew word.

A few minutes later, from a tenebrous calle we walked into the bright light and dazzling space of the Piazza San Marco. Hearing music, we walked into the square and stood behind the last row of outdoor tables of the Cafe Lavena. The five-piece band on the raised bandstand had finished one set of popular Italian tunes and then, all of a sudden, began playing familiar melodies, the Jewish songs I had heard them play once before. I raised my hand and waved to the clarinetist. He saw me and, while playing, lifted his instrument, acknowledging my greeting.

"Do you know this music?" I asked Gila.

She shook her head. "Do you know him?" she wrote. "He seems to know you."

"There's a story behind this, Gila. Listen. A few days ago I was here, standing in the same spot — by the way, this Cafe dates back to 1750 — and all of a sudden the musicians begin to play some popular Jewish and Hebrew tunes. People start clapping and dancing in place. I see an Arab lady next to me clapping and swaying, not realizing, of course, that she's being delighted by a popular Israeli song. When the musicians took a break, I went up to the bandstand and began chatting with the clarinetist. I asked him how he knew these tunes and he told me he comes from Kishinev, and he learned these songs from some Jewish musician friends. So now that he saw me standing here he began this set of Jewish songs for you and me and I waved my thanks to him.... Would you like to sit down here for a drink or an ice cream?"

Gila shook her head. Instead of writing she put one fist atop the other and began to make the gondolier's rowing movements.

"You read my mind," I said. "That's just what I was about to suggest. Let's wait until this set of tunes is over and then we'll go."

A few minutes later I waved to the clarinetist as Gila took my arm again and we made our way out of the square. Soon we stood in front of a gondolier's station by a narrow canal. We walked down three stone steps to the side of a gondola.

The gondolier, a handsome chap in his early forties, deeply tanned from his hours in the sun, helped Gila and then me down into the gondola. As is the custom for the forty-minute ride, I paid the man his hefty fee in advance. Gila sat down on the left red plush cushion and leaned back into the equally comfortable pillow. I did the same. Then I looked at her and said with a smile, "A gentleman always sits to the left of a lady on a gondola." So we switched seats. "Now we are official Venice tourists," I said, and I put my arm around her shoulder.

She nestled into my embrace; her first sign of expressed affection, and a spurt of *gila* went through me. Walking arm in arm through the calles, I considered just stylishly Old World. But this I took quite naturally and made no comment to her. And why I had concocted that scenario about a gentleman sitting to the left of a woman on a gondola I do not know. I thought about it afterward but can't explain it. As it turned out, it was good that I sat to her left.

The gondolier, from his perch behind us, propelled the gondola forward. I hadn't realized until I was in one how big and long the gondola was. And it took some strength to row it, and with only one oar too.

Curt Leviant

Wouldn't it be exciting, I thought, if I would see someone I knew from the community as we rode along the canal? While I remained still, relaxed, on the gondola with Gila, Venice floated by, as if I were sitting home and watching a huge video of the city with all its colorful buildings and little bridges enveloping me. If I see anyone, ran through my mind, it would be Roni doing his daily run. Him I wouldn't mind seeing me with Gila. It would show him that someone was interested in the lonely mute woman whom everyone shunned, perhaps because of her impediment, perhaps because they didn't know what to say to her, or how to say the things they were reticent of saying. Roni seeing me with Gila would also serve another purpose. It would show the rabbi I wasn't interested in Mazal.

But wait! What am I talking about? Roni never even had an inkling that I was attracted to Mazal. On the contrary, if anything, *he* was the one who may have been attracted to her. And doubly on the contrary: from his point of view I had a disdain for Mazal's primitive religiosity, her superstitions, her pagan desire to go to the Padua cemetery and prostrate herself on the grave of a long dead rabbi to beseech help. My entire speechify longishly, as Mazal put it so charmingly, clearly showed that for me she wasn't at all an object of desire. Maybe Umberto dei Rossi knew it, but Roni didn't.

For the table top in Roni's dining room was an excellent divider, a superb creator of masks and disguises, a fine fence of separation. That Formica or faux wood divider lets you reveal what's going on above the table but cloaks perfectly the below-the-table lusts and impulses.

Had I seen Roni running I would have waved to him; even more, I would have shouted, Roni, shalom!

From down in a gondola Venice looked different. The buildings, the palazzos, glide by. When one walks in Venice, the buildings take on the walker's pace. But once you're way down in a gondola, especially in a narrow canal, the buildings, as if on water skis, sail quickly toward you.

We moved in that almost waltz-like rhythm of the gondola's forward flow. Other gondoliers achieved a dance rhythm of their own with a forward bend, relax, straighten up, then lean forward again. Although the ride was always smooth, I sensed an undercurrent of a hesitation in our path through the canals.

Gila looked with obvious delight at the grand palazzos on the Grand Canal. She enjoyed too the tiny canals and the many arched bridges where — and here she turned to look — where our gondolier had to duck down as he sailed under the bridge. To the tourists on the little bridges, watching the parade of gondolas one after the other and waving, Gila waved back. She opened her mouth with surprise as she heard the gondolier sing out the warning "Oh-yee, oh-yee" as he was about to round a sharp corner.

With Gila's more sensitive hearing she no doubt enjoyed the sound of the oar in the water and the lap lap of the man-created waves.

I felt like a prince, perhaps a duke, as the studied rhythm — deep dip, then two smaller dips — swept us smoothly through the water. The gondolier's movements were musical, and their repeated gestures, like melodies, leitmotifs in compositions. Now he took us along a very narrow canal, and I preferred that to riding on the broad Grand Canal crowded with vaporettos, snub-nosed transport crafts, and motorboats.

Just as we were approaching one of the small stone footbridges that spanned our canal, I saw, my God, I couldn't believe

Curt Leviant

it, Mazal walking across the bridge. She didn't look my way, but I was so surprised, yes, and agitated too, that she might see me with Gila, that I ducked, and fearing a collision with the soon-to-come stone bridge, quickly twisted to the left, shouted "Down" to Gila, and covered my face with my right hand.

My sudden shift caused —

But before I tell you what happened I have to describe the unique shape of the gondola. Think of a huge elongated oval about thirty-six feet long and four feet wide in the middle, and then add a subtle inward twist on the right front and the left rear. Because of this asymmetry the gondolier stands at the rear of the gondola, slightly to the left of center, and needs only one oar to row.

I don't know the physics to account for this. Perhaps the gondolier knows and, more likely, the gondola maker can explain it. In any case, the gondola's design is scientifically and very carefully configured and perfect balance is essential.

That's why my sudden shift in the gondola caused a problem.

Suddenly, a cry from the gondolier, a guttural shout from the man who had been silent till now. Remember, this canal was quite narrow, with room for just one gondola and about three feet to spare on either side. And since we were now some twenty-five feet away from a little bridge, the gondolier also had to shift from standing to bending down. But because of my sudden movements, the gondola's precarious balance was suddenly compromised and it rocked from side to side. The gondolier's attempt to balance himself by touching the wall of the building to his right made the gondola rock even more. Before I knew it I tumbled into the shallow water. But I quickly stood and waded two or three strides to the stone steps that led to the sidewalk.

Gila was still in the gondola, holding on — it was good that we had switched seats — and the gondolier was cursing in Venetian dialect. Practiced in his craft and with balletic grace, he managed to right himself. Then he braked with his oar, turned the gondola sharply to the left and guided it back to the steps I had just used. In a rage, he shouted to Gila, "Off. Off. Out!"

I took Gila's hand and led her up to the sidewalk. At the edge people bent forward to help us up.

Meanwhile, the gondolier was shouting at me, in English. "No keep your balance, hah? Sink in canal to take bath." And then, laughing, he imitated a person losing his balance and rowed away, still hurling Italian curses at us.

And he hadn't even given us the forty minutes.

In contrast to the gondolier, the people on the little sidewalk were so nice, Venetians and tourists alike. After helping us, they stood at the edge of the sidewalk and asked us if we were okay.

At first, Gila hadn't shown any reaction to the gondolier's impudence. For a moment she stood there, immobile. Then she stretched out her right hand and, with a grim expression on her face, pointed toward the gondolier. As if Gila were calling to him, he turned. Once again, she jabbed her index finger twice at him as though berating him, or sending imprecations his way. The gondolier stood immobile, still facing us. And then, to our astonishment, his gondola approached the stone bridge and the gondolier crashed into it. He hit it with his back and the blow knocked him into the water while his gondola took off without him.

The onlookers applauded.

"These gondoliers," I heard a man say, "they think they're the doges of Venice."

Could this have been Gila's doing? Maybe, but I didn't want to ask her as yet. The shock of my falling into the water and the sudden end to our gondola ride was still too fresh.

But I did ask her: "Were you scared when the gondola began shaking and I fell out?"

Gila shook her head.

But, you know, I also remember that scene this way:

During that ride occurred one of those events you read about in the local paper and go, "Tsk, tsk," in commiseration, and then turn to the sports pages.

It was my fault.

Our gondolier was approaching a little bridge. Standing behind us, he called out a warning in English, "Bridge coming. Plenty room. But still, lean back."

I looked up at the bridge and thought I saw Mazal crossing it.

With the sheer surprise of this, and not wanting her to see me at all costs, without thinking I put my arm over my face and instead of leaning back I suddenly, can't explain it, suddenly twisted to my left to avoid being seen, and with the gondolier ducking too the careful balance of the gondola was upset.

Next thing I knew it capsized, and all three of us were in the water. The gondolier, cursing in Venetian, had just managed to grab hold of his gondola, while his oar was taking a straight course under the bridge.

While he cried out, "Where my oar?" I, not seeing Gila, was shouting, "Where's Gila?"

Then I heard the gondolier mutter, "She floats like log, like wooden oar, next to my oar."

Now I'm not a good swimmer. In fact, I can't swim at all — and I've always had a fear of water. Me, I'm the sort that can drown in a tub. But in the very narrow and shallow canal, I was able to wade to the three stone steps that led up to the sidewalk. And then a man ran up to the gondolier and handed him his oar, at which the gondolier said, "Grazie. Grazie mille."

I apologized to the gondolier, but he turned his back. Since I had already paid him in advance, I left, running along the narrow sidewalk at the length of the canal, dripping wet.

Where could Gila have gone? I replayed the gondolier's comment: she's floating like a log. I wanted to ask passersby if they had seen someone floating here but it sounded so ridiculous I kept still and continued running. Then I saw her, standing on the narrow sidewalk, her hair glistening. I was so happy to see her safe I ran up and threw my arms around her and for the first time kissed her cheek.

For a couple of minutes we stood in the sunshine and I let the warm rays dry my clothes. I kept apologizing to Gila for what had happened, but she gestured and made faces to say it was all right, don't worry.

"Come," I said, "we'll find a cafe and have a hot drink."

Gila took out her pad and wrote:

"What made you twist and turn like that?"

I thought quickly and said, "I was afraid we would bump into the bridge, and I wanted you to bend down too."

Luckily, this incident had occurred after Mazal had crossed the bridge. Ma wasn't even aware of it and was likely deep into the calle, oblivious to what had happened with us.

For a few minutes we walked along the narrow sidewalk that overlooked the canal and found a cafe at the very edge, near another bridge.

"This must be the smallest cafe in the universe," I said. It was a tiny hole in the wall, with two little wrought iron tables outside, which left just a bit of room for passersby to make their way forward. I had never been to this area of Venice. Further down there were two more small bridges.

"Would you like a cappuccino?" I asked her.

"I don't drink coffee," she wrote. "But tea would be fine."

This little place obviously did not have a waiter. It was self-service.

"I'll get you a cup of tea in a minute." I said. "Tell me, what kind of message did you send the gondolier when you pointed at him? You pointed once, and then a moment later jabbed your index finger twice at him, as if berating him for his nasty behavior."

And Gila wrote, "No no. I just wanted to alert him to the bridge that was quickly coming."

I looked at her with a bit of disbelief, but in her eye, either the chartreuse or the lavender, I don't recall, I saw a victorious little smile.

I drew my chair closer to hers. I stretched out my hands and held her face. Felt the three letters of *Shabbat* vibrating in my left palm. Perhaps those tremors went into her face too. Gila looked at me, not with surprise, not anticipation. But the color in each eye was deeper, richer than ever before. I didn't bring my face close to hers. With someone else I would have done it slowly, looking into her eyes. With Gila I didn't know what to expect. Had I moved slowly she might have stretched out her hand and gently rebuffed me. With her I wanted to move quickly.

I raised my hand and showed her the three letters for Shabbat, now darker than usual, throbbing on my left palm. Up to this time I had not kissed her. I did not even think of inviting her to my apartment. There was something virginal, ascetic, brotherly-sisterly about our relationship, which made me recall that enigmatic two-word phrase from the Song of Songs, *akhoti kala*, "my sister, my bride." But yet that *Shabbat* was pulsing on my palm, going to its own rhythm, as though totally removed from me. Gila looked at it. Made a motion as if striking a match.

"Burning, huh?" I said.

She nodded, then surprised me.

Gila took my hand, spread my fingers, raised my palm to her mouth and kissed the word *Shabbat*, the three letters she herself had imprinted in me. Soon as she did this I seized her, put my arms around her, and kissed her lips.

She sighed, just like Mazal did when I held her shoulder with Gila's *Shabbat* pressing against her skin, but Gila's exhaling was long and silent, as though one soul were going through her, and her intake of breath was equally long, as though a new soul had entered her.

I kissed her lips, her sweet full lips. She brought her arms around me and held the back of my head. I had not realized how full her lips were because I was so taken by her face, especially her eyes, one lavender, the other chartreuse, that I had not taken the time, like a movie camera slowly panning over the heroine's face, to focus on each feature of her handsome, yes, handsome, that's the elusive word I had been looking for to describe her un-usual beauty, yes, her handsome face.

As I kissed her deeper, I felt something in her mouth. Couldn't tell what.

Then, suddenly, I sensed, and I mean suddenly, but this tri-syllabic word is turtle slow in its labyrinthine pace compared to the lightning swift suddenness, that shutter speed quick sudden sensation I felt when I tasted that spurt of ecstasy that jolt of ecstasy, that Adam felt when he first kissed Eve, that my palm felt when that first letter of *Shabbat*, the *shin*, ש, was etched into my hand, the *shin* that is also the first letter of God's name, Shaddai, that Moses felt when he saw the flame in the bramble bush the flame there but the bush not consumed, as I was with her singe of fire that went through all my limbs like an elixir, a magic potion that seared my nerves, my bones, my lips as I placed my lips on hers.

When she opened her eyes for a moment the lilac blue lavender of one eye suddenly deepened. It became a deep stained glass liquidy blue, the spectacular shiny blue of lapis lazuli.

I thought I heard an Oh from her but I didn't hear an Oh. I thought my heart would pound but my heart did not pound. But I tasted sweetness, a rose-flavored honey on my lips, my fingertips. I felt I could write Hebrew letters and imprint them on someone else's palm. And then, oh what was that, how un-glorious, un-ecstatic, was that tiny sharp-edged piece of stiff paper or plastic in her mouth? Oh no! The tiny something I had felt before. A loose tooth? I felt it after that electric elixir had faded and there was a hint, oh just a minuscule hint of a smile in Gila's eyes but not on her lips.

I wanted to ask her, did she have a loose tooth that perhaps she wasn't aware of. Or a sliver of a broken cap? But why embarrass her. I had learned my lesson with Mazal. A buttoned lip is a boon for gracious social intercourse.

Now that I had kissed her I was prepared to consider a very personal question I wouldn't have dreamt of asking her before. Was she born with that vocal problem? Or was it an illness? For usually people who are mute are deaf too. Nevertheless, although I felt more at ease with Gila, I still reined in my curiosity and kept silent. I couldn't ask the question I wanted to ask. Or had she pointed her index finger at me too and mesmerized me like she had mesmerized the gondolier to crash into the stone bridge?

At first I was sure that I had indeed kissed her lips. But then I wasn't, like an old man who thinks he has found his glasses but finds only an empty case. I still don't know if the kiss was real or a dream. Ever since that three-lettered *Shabbat* was indited into my palms — but why talk in passive. Ever since Gila had written that *Shabbat* into my palm the border between what I experienced with her and what I imagined was fuzzy. At times I was absolutely sure of an event; but later it had a vague watery feel, totally unfocused, and it seemed to me that I had dreamt it. Like the two varying scenes on the gondola, when I saw Mazal crossing the bridge.

That kiss felt strong and powerful. I am still surprised at the rich, luxuriant fullness of her lips, for she didn't seem to have full lips. But then it played in my memory and I thought, why should she kiss me? Likely she did not.

I watched the water in the canal. It kept changing colors, reflecting the clothes of the people passing by. Gila and I had been in the water together. I wondered if there was something symbolic about this. Like the opposite of passing through fire. We passed through water. Came out of the water. Reborn. Was I bound to her? I wondered.

She lifted her finger, a sign she wanted to say, write, something. She went into her bag and took out her little pad.

"Words bind us," Gila wrote.

But I had just thought that word "bound". You read my mind, I didn't say. And to myself I repeated those three words. First she gives me three letters, now she gives me three words. Again three words. Like before, when she had written: only on yours.

I've said before, I love three-word sentences, noun, verb,

something else. They have a proverbial, even a prophetic ring. I read those three words not as an abstract philosophical observation, where the *us* is a synonym for people in general. I read the *us* as me and you, and I liked that, for I saw it as an expression of affection. And I liked it too because that three-word sentence sent a synoptic message. It had crispness and compressed wisdom.

Her short line was noun, verb, pronoun. She probably didn't realize that her remark sent a double message. It upside-downed itself, like in a convex lens. That little sentence radiated two thoughts. And the key to that double meaning was not the noun, not the pronoun. It was the mirror slippery verb in the middle.

When Gila wrote, "Words bind us," she was no doubt referring to the word *Shabbat* that she had given me that now linked both of us. But in the convex mirror "bind" also means "ties", in the sense that words tie us up, restrict our freedom, confuse us, cause problems, bind us. Words put us into a bind. Especially when I forget to button my lip.

"In any language," I added. "Tell me, Gila, you seem so sensitive to words and language, how many languages do you know?"

She wrote: "Spanish, Hebrew, English, and a bit ..." But then I saw her delete the last three words.

I wanted to know her first language. "Which language were you born into?"

Gila hesitated, thought a moment, then circled around the question by writing: "I was raised in Spanish and Hebrew."

Soon as I heard Spanish, that man I had named Mo came into my thoughts. He too with his Spanish-tinged English knew Spain. Could it be that in this tiny town Mo and Mu did not know each other? Then, at once, the title of my unwritten, but now unfolding, book appeared again: *Me, Mo, Mu, Ma & Mod*, with the latter holding up a sign he himself had made, a two-by-two white placard with only a bright red question mark on it. Had Leone da Modena known Yiddish he could had written a tiny word that rhymes with Mu—Nu? Signifying: Well? Aren't you going to write about *me*? Or, do I really need to be sidelined by Ma and Mu?

Yes, Mu knows three languages, but I didn't hear anything from her pertaining to culture, books, the arts, the lively little world I inhabited. At least Mazal, because of her problems, discussed religious tradition, folk customs, which I call superstitions, and belief.

When I concluded Gila had to be smart because she knew three languages, another thought in me rebutted: simple, uneducated, uncultivated men who lived in lands with shifting borders and had experienced the exigencies of war, dislocation and migration, also spoke and understood several languages. I had met people like that. But that wasn't necessarily a marker of culture. Those people probably could not read the literature of the languages they spoke, nor did they know the cultural history of those lands. Their knowledge of those languages was superficial and skimpy. Moreover, I had to remind myself that it was much easier to communicate with Mazal. And I really hadn't had a chance to do any serious talking with Gila. So, as you can see, I'm going here and there, back and forth. Ma and Mu.

When I asked Gila about her childhood and her parents, she dismissed these questions with a curt, "I don't have an interesting past."

I was about to tell her, I'm sure you do, but I just said, "Have you traveled?"

"Mostly in Spain," she wrote. Had she spoken I would have

noticed a nostalgic tone to her voice. But given her silence, I saw it on her face. "I saw the famous old Jewish cities: Toledo, Cordova, Granada. And then, on my way here, through south France and north Italy."

"Then you were born in Spain."

"You might say that," she wrote, but there was an enigmatic, coy little light in her lavender chartreuse eyes.

Did she mean she was born on the border of Spain and France, a region claimed by both countries? Or Spain and Portugal? Or was it an island near Spain whose ownership was in dispute?

As I was preparing to ask her another question, I saw that Gila was watching another gondolier make his rhythmic dance movements as he steered his gondola. She took a sip of the tea in front of her and gave me a little smile. That little smile made me happy. I wanted to bend forward and kiss her again — but I waited.

"And where did you get your education?"

I watched her type. She typed very slowly and I, by temperament impatient, had to cork my restlessness and wait until her lugubrious one-finger typing was done.

"Mostly self-educated," she wrote. "I really started serious learning as a young adult."

A few minutes earlier, regarding language, I saw that she had deleted a couple of words. Now I saw her fingers hovering over her tiny keyboard; then, apparently changing her mind, she moved it away.

Then Gila started asking me questions, typing very slowly.

"Talk all about yourself," she wrote. "What was. What is. What will be. So I wouldn't have to type questions every few minutes. Schooling. Did you study music? Singing? You have such a melodic speaking voice. What ambitions do, did, you have?"

I couldn't figure it out. Did she really want to know all about me, or was she doing this to avoid talking any more about herself? Because by Gila typing in one question after another, especially one that needed a long answer, I was deflected from asking her more about herself. After a while I got the hint. When I saw that my questions made her uncomfortable, especially about her early life, I desisted.

And maybe that's why she typed so slowly. Was this andante linked to her reluctance to answer personal questions? Or was it because this was a new gadget and she was working in a language that wasn't her native tongue?

And I answered her questions. In my own way. Giving some facts about myself. Embellishing others. The embellishments were more fun. I told her my ambition was to become a composer. Like Mozart, I wrote my first piano concerto when I was six months old. I didn't smile when I said this. Neither did she. I did sing early on. I was a six-year-old baritone and my voice never changed. I sang Schubert lieder and set to music a snippet of one of the two or three Hebrew poems I knew by the great eleventh century poet and philosopher, Shlomo ibn Gvirol, who lived in Spain. And I thought: there's that "mo" sound again.

That last name must have impressed her for she gave a start, a little forward motion of her body, almost as if she wanted to make a comment on this. But she did not go to her little pad. I guess she was touched somehow by my remark about the famous Hebrew poet. Then I quickly continued, saying that when I saw I wasn't successful in musical composition, I switched from notes to words, composing with alphabetical instead of musical symbols. That went well for me, I said. But I still love music. I know

Curt Leviant

the entire classical repertoire. For instance, I can sing the first note of almost every well-known classical composition, from Bach to Mozart and Beethoven through Tchaikovsky, Bloch and Gershwin. I exercise every day. Play baseball. Do you know what baseball is? No? Okay, imagine a gondolier's oar. You hold it up like this, someone throws a ball at you and you swing, like this, and try to hit the ball and then you start running.

"Running away?" she typed. "Because you're afraid?"

"No. Running to. Because you're exhilarated. It's part of the game."

Gila shook her and wrote, "Ridiculous."

I saw it her way. "You're right. Absolutely ridiculous. And sometimes fifty thousand people fill a huge stadium to watch people who get millions of dollars every year to do this ridiculous thing."

And then, looking at her admiringly, I added, "What kind of magic power do you have, Gila?" And, saying this, I felt a surge in me, as if her magic power was even stronger now that I had said those two words, even adding a 'd' into power to make it even more magical, and all kinds of chemicals that control emotive sensations rose up in me in this surge, "....that you can get me to talk about myself. I usually don't tell anybody anything about myself. Recently, someone brazenly asked me, How old are you? I said at once, I don't answer personal questions. But with you everything in me seems to flow so naturally out of me toward you, as if there is a stream between us that takes this flow and I actually feel it's a pleasure giving you autobiographical facts. Usually, I don't speechify so longishly, as a foreign friend remarked recently, and more, usually I'm the one who asks and it's the other person who speechifies longishly at my prodding, while I'm the one who remains silent and listens carefully, remembering almost nothing of consequence and everything of no consequence."

"Why haven't you married?" Gila suddenly asked me. I watched her artistocratic fingers — I meant to say "aristocratic", but I see that my neologism makes sense too — as one of them, her index finger, typed the words.

"I never found anyone I wanted to spend the rest of my life with."

Until now, a pressure within, or without, me pushed me to say. Maybe it was her magic. A little ditty danced on the fringe of my consciousness. Four words based on her eyes, one lavender, the other chartreuse. "Two different eyes mesmerize." Or maybe it was her *Shabbat* on my palm that pulsed me to think *until now*. But I didn't speak. I buttoned my lip and held it tight. No use getting into an emotional mess, a perhaps inextricable situation, by blurting out two compromising words.

Her sudden question elicited another question in me. Her question should have been the second in a series of two, the first of which was, Are you married? But she asked the second one first.

"And, by the way, how do you know I never married," I said, looking into one eye and then the other. "You didn't ask me, Are you married? You said, why haven't you married? How do you know I wasn't once married?"

"I know. I can tell," she wrote, and again there was a little, the tiniest of smiles in her eyes.

"How?"

She raised her enchanting two-hued eyes up to the sky, as if the answer would be there in one of the low hanging clouds. "You have that hungry look," is what she typed.

For a moment we gazed at each other. Did this glance have the warmth of people who knew each other, liked each other, formed a bond? Or was it the look of people who are merely acquainted and can't take the mighty, potent, binding electric current of four eyes locked into each other, where soon enough one set of eyes can't take the intimate, soul-stirring stare and one turns away?

"Are you word composing now?" Gila asked.

"You mean at this very moment?"

"I mean now, in Venice."

"Even now, at this very moment, I am word composing in my thoughts, and the words I am writing are, 'He leaned over the table,' as I am doing now, 'and he kissed her delicious full lips.'"

Which I did and to which she responded by moving her chair closer. But this time I did not feel that little tiny thing in her mouth. I held her lower lip between mine for a moment and savored the taste that seemed to run time through me.

I looked at Gila and said, "I had a project to write about Leone da Modena. A unique and fascinating man...Have you heard of him?"

She nodded.

But since that project was fading in my mind, I did not tell her that I was now writing about people I had just met.

"You have delicious lips," I told her. "When I kiss you, strange feelings run through me. As if an hour glass were reversed in me and I can taste centuries running through me, filling me, dizzying me. I feel I could have stepped out in Leone da Modena's time."

She opened her little pad.

"I have a confession to make."

Gila looked down shyly.

"Okay. If you want to share it with me."

And she wrote: "I have never been kissed before."

I looked at her, astonished. I didn't say I don't believe you. That would have been impudent and insensitive. But why would a grown woman admit this if it weren't so? Still, it was hard to believe that such delicious lips hadn't ever been kissed. And then through me ran the thought: that's a very intimate revelation she has shared with me, a very heartfelt confession.

"And is this the first time I've kissed you?"

But Gila just smiled. Another question she didn't answer.

Then, instead of asking her the question I really wanted to ask her about her muteness, I said:

"I'm curious about you, Gila. You don't talk much about yourself." I smiled hesitantly, aware of the verb I had just used. "You know what I mean."

"I told you, not interesting," she wrote. "I'm just a small speck in this vast universe."

"So am I," I said. Even smaller, I thought. "But still I want to know where you come from. What you do. Are you working here? On some kind of mission?"

"You're more interesting," she replied, typing slowly. "What are you doing here?"

At least she didn't ask me, like I asked Mo, when I met him right after I had entered the Ghetto: Why are you here?

"Didn't I tell you? I was invited by the Jewish community here as a writer, in honor of the Ghetto's five hundredth anniversary." And then I asked Gila another question about something that irked me.

"Where do you live, Gila? You always seem to disappear."

She didn't answer.

"Can't you tell me?"

She shook her head. Then she wrote: "Private."

Curt Leviant

That hurt, that word. But I wouldn't let that dissuade me. Maybe she lived with someone and that's why she was so secretive about her address. Or maybe it was on account of modesty, so she wouldn't be tempted to invite me in. It wasn't until much later that I became aware of another reason.

Her one-word response jolted me out of the swift-moving hour glass of time and I felt I was done for today with Gila. For a moment my sense of pride was compromised and I told myself, That's it. No more with her today. But still I found myself saying:

"Let's meet again."

"Gladly," she wrote.

"I want to take you to the Lido. Have you been there?"

She wrote, "No. But I'd like to see the famous old Jewish cemetery where all the notable Jews from previous centuries have been buried."

"Yes," I said, "including Leone da Modena, who was born here and served as rabbi here."

I wasn't too keen on going to the Lido cemetery, but I would take her, especially since it wasn't a religious quest with superstitious overtones. Then it struck me. Two women, two cemeteries. Too much. What's going on here?

"Next Sunday," she wrote.

"So long to wait?" I said sadly.

"Can't."

"In the morning I look for you," I said.

Gila's eyes open wide in surprise. Then she wrote, "Did you purposely say that?"

"Well, I don't talk accidentally," I said, somewhat peeved.

"I mean, do you know those words are a title of a poem?"

"No. Whose?"

"By that poet you mentioned before, part of whose poem you set to music. Shlomo Ibn Gvirol."

"No kidding." Again Mo, I thought. "What a coincidence."

"There are no coincidences," Gila wrote.

"I really don't know his work. I just knew a few lines from two or three poems."

"And the poem, 'In the Morning I Look for You', is actually a kind of prayer, addressed not to a woman but to God."

"Okay," I said. "I'll look for Him too in the morning. Maybe He will help me look for you."

"But you did find me," Gila wrote.

And I thought, Yes, I found you, but I really didn't *find* you.

We made up to meet at the Lido in front of the Grand Hotel, the one made famous by Thomas Mann's *Death in Venice*. I thought of mentioning this to her but she probably didn't know Thomas Mann and I didn't want to appear to be showing off.

"Will I see you in the synagogue Friday night or *Shabbat* morning? Or at the Kiddush?"

"I don't know. I may not be there."

"But on Sunday you'll be in front of the hotel, or in the lobby if it rains, right?"

"Yes. Yes," she wrote.

Then she took out a piece of paper and began to write on it with her pen. When she finished she handed it to me.

"Why didn't you type it?" I asked.

And she continued with the pen. "Because I want you to have it."

This is what she wrote:

"If it comes about, there may come a time and I will give you something made by a famous person from long ago."

Curt Leviant

"That's so nice of you," I said, thinking: well, that's a broad category. Had she said artist or sculptor I might have been able to narrow it down. I read the lines again; I looked at Gila. She didn't acknowledge the fantastic contents of her remark with a smile or a nod, to somehow affirm her words with a facial gesture. No. Her face remained austere. Her note would have made a greater impact had she smiled or shown some emotive sign. Without this the words seemed disembodied. Still, there was a buried treasure intrigue to her alluring promise.

After re-reading her words, I exclaimed:

"What? You have such an artifact?"

Using a word from the vocabulary of archeology I felt awkward, as awkward as that word itself, the only word in the English language with the "wkw" combination and the palindromic "awk wa" form. But what could I say? Perhaps it wasn't a painting or a sculpture crafted out of precious metal, marble or wood. Could I assume it was a manuscript? A book?

The questions bubbled out of me, but not before I spoke of worth.

"If from long ago such an item is priceless. How did it come into your possession? Did you buy it? Inherit it?" I asked, even though I knew she would not answer.

Gila did not. She put the pen down. I gazed at it and at her, assuming that by sheer force of will I could urge her, persuade her, con her to tell me more. A stubborn look came over her pretty face, which apparently couldn't express many nuances.

Except for her green eye. Other people, all their features, even nose and cheeks, relay thoughts and feeling. With Gila it was one eye. When excited or moved, her eyelid narrowed and the chartreuse turned a deeper green, like an oak leaf in June, the eye that radiated all-knowing shrewdness. A calculating eye, scheming with possibilities. But this seemingly tough side of her was mitigated by the azure country innocence of her blue eye that held the other one in check, like a counterweight.

For a moment Gila put her right index finger to her lips. Had she kept it there for a moment or two I would have concluded that she was saying, Yes, it's a secret. But that motion was so fleeting and so ambiguous I couldn't interpret it that way. Neither did I ask her: Is it a secret for now?

Her vague written promise prompted me later to imagine a fantastic scenario that had floated through my mind before: Two strange creatures in the ghetto; both had links to Spain and both knew Hebrew. Maybe they knew each other. I go back to Mo's house and, to my shock, Gila opens the door. She says Mo is not at home and welcomes me in. Oh my God, I thought, she's related to him. Maybe his wife. Although I had never seen them together. So I decided to ask her, Are you Mo's wife? No, she said. Girl friend? Again came her, No. Then what? I continued. Yes, she said.

But I realized I had only thought these questions; didn't dare to ask them out loud.

Before I folded her note and put it into my pocket I reprised her promise, if promise it was, and read it again. Sometimes a few reviews are needed for an impact to settle in. What did it mean, *There may come a time*? What kind of cockamamie promise is that? *There may come a time*. Either you give a gift or you don't. Was there a certain condition that had to be met and if I didn't meet it she wouldn't give it? Would I have to accomplish a fairytale challenge? I had never ever heard of such a queer formulation: *There may come a time*. That slippery monosyllable, *may*. But I wasn't going to spoil her remark or argue about something that did not yet exist.

We said good-bye. I knew by now not to insist on accompanying her home. I did not kiss her lips but I hugged her and pressed my face to hers and kissed her cheek, and it seemed to me that she kissed my cheek too, for a line of warmth went through my cheeks into my mouth and tongue, a little bite of fire. That bite is written correctly. It's not that I meant to write *bit* and it came out *bite*. I wrote *bite* and meant it. A moment's bite of fire.

"I'll be seeing you pretty soon. Good-bye," I whispered into her ear. And in forming the letters I brushed my lips in kiss-like fashion in her ear.

"Next Sunday," she wrote. "A week from today."

As soon as we parted, it didn't take too long before another young woman overwhelmed me, it's not as if I forgot Gila, but for a moment she was overshadowed, Mu to Ma, and the first thing I thought of was Mazal coming to my apartment tomorrow. I couldn't believe it. I was split down the middle with Mazal. Picturing her, little rills of heat spiraled up in me. Her radiant Eros was even stronger by the park bench than in the rabbi's apartment. But yet I had argued with her, criticized her, disagreed with her primitive views. After that Friday night dinner at Roni's I never dreamt she'd fall into my lap the way she did. I didn't know what to expect, but my bones, my skin, were sending indeterminate messages in alphabets I could not decipher.

On my way home I saw him running again. Who? Roni, the running rabbi. I looked at him. Funny — strange, rather — how the same face looks different if a certain event has intervened. It was my meeting with Mazal after that Friday night dinner that changed Roni's face. Actually, my perception of it skewed the skittery nerves that controlled my eyes. This was happening, it seemed to me, only because of my private encounter with him. It might have been different had I seen him with other people. And why, I now wondered, was he running around Venice, like pious Jews of old would circumstroll the walls of Jerusalem, either before or after prayers? Was there something more to it than mere exercise? Was it kabbalistic? Mystical?

Although I wasn't sure about his relationship with Mazal, I felt guilty, assuming I might be consorting with his girl friend. In fact, had I stopped Roni he likely would have asked about her — by power of that special insight, or soul reading, that Hasidic rebbes have, even though this Israeli Yemenite was miles away from being a Polish Hasidic rebbe. In Hasidic circles it's called "the look", that all-knowing, penetrating glance that drills into you and sees everything. And I was prepared to confess. To tell him I had met Mazal by chance near the entrance to the Biennale. But I certainly would not discuss with him my inviting her to my apartment. Or her ready consent. Confession after a "look" goes only so far. And there are limits to self-immolation.

9   Modena in My Dream

I had been at the tipping point of dropping my plan to write about
Leone da Modena and Venice. But the day I met Mazal I decided
to abandon it, at least for now. It's always easier to postpone than
come to a definitive conclusion. Don't forget that I had also seen
Mazal and the mute woman on Sunday. Ma and Mu on one day.
And at one point had even seen both at the same time. And these
two surely overshadowed poor old Leone. They were here and
now, while Mod was there and then.

As if to make his presence felt, and apparently having eaves-
dropped on Mazal's excursus on dreams, that night Modena came
to me, unbidden, in a dream   and furious he was too. During the
day, when one receives visitors, a certain protocol is followed. Call
it social grace. You invite, he accepts. On the given day he rings
your bell you welcome him in. He offers a gift you didn't want,
a gift he didn't want to bring. "You shouldn't have," you say, the
only true words in the entire exchange, as you look with eyes full
of false admiration at the useless thing now in your hands. "But I
wanted to," he lies.

Sleep, however, changes the protocol. Gone good manners.

Leone da Modena appeared, no knock needed. Commenced
at once his vituperative complaint.

"What?" was his first word. Uttered, and fortissimo too, even
before he crossed the threshold.

Modena (1571-1648), somewhat short, about 5'6", bur erect
and dignified, looked just like the late 16th century man I had

imagined him to be. He saluted me awkwardly, putting his palm to his old-fashioned reddish brown peaked hat. I noted his bright, clever brown eyes, the alert eyes of a card player and gambler, sharp, roving, never still, under slightly tense brows. He had a small beard and wore a collarless jacket, a white ruffled scarf and a thick belt with a big silver buckle and tapered dark blue trousers, more accurately, knickers. I didn't get a chance to look at his shoes — likely they were boots — for at once he continued morosely:

"You don't know how happy I was that someone finally remembered me, wanted to write about my exciting, memorable life. And now, suddenly, you've suddenly dropped me.... Why?" he whined.

I wasn't about to obey the wise Yiddish expression: the truth is the best lie....and say: Because I found a better subject. For that would be hurtful, so I decided to say:

"I have to do some juggling," were the words that suddenly came to me. "I haven't abandoned you. I'm expanding the project. I will include you, I promise."

Thus said, for even in dreams one must be polite and considerate.

"B...b...better," he sputtered. "What do you mean better? What could be better than my story? My inimitable autobiography? For your information, here are...."

Only in dreams can a visitor uncover cover-ups so quickly and read the dreamer's mind.

"....some details of which I will remind you and the rest I'll give you another time....How many rabbis do you know who had so many professions: cantor, poet, writer of comedies, matchmaker, commercial agent, gambler, secretary of charitable organizations, sermon writer, calligrapher, translator, writer of amulets? And these are just some...”

The next morning I saw a sheet of paper on my desk. At first I thought it was mine, written unawares during sleep, a phenomenon known as automatic writing. But when I looked closely I saw a sheet of old paper. And the handwriting, a neat hand-calligraphed Torah script, wasn't mine either. Upon reading it I realized it was a list of Modena's occupations and professions.

Leone da Modena had kept his promise. But he didn't leave a contact number.

There was only one way to check if this was indeed Modena's handwriting, or if some ghostly pal was playing a trick on me. I took the morning train to Parma and made my way to the University of Parma Library, which had one of the most magnificent collections of rare Hebrew manuscripts in the world. In the rare manuscripts room I asked to see their handwritten copy of Modena's *Kol Sakhal*, The Voice of a Fool, Mod's sly attack on ultra-orthodox Judaism during his time. Leone cleverly used the old ruse — of discovering a manuscript supposedly written by someone else and publishing it as a public service.

I asked their calligraphic expert to compare my sheet of paper with their copy of *Kol Sakhal*. The answer was astounding. The old scholar concluded it's the same handwriting.

“May I congratulate you? You have a rare and valuable treasure in your possession,” the man said. “A page with Leone da Modena's handwriting, and signed by him! There are not many extant in the world. I hope if you ever decide to donate it you will think of us. It would be a valuable addition to our collection. Only problem with it is—it's difficult to date.”

I thanked him and said I would certainly consider it.

Well, I kept my promise to Leone da Modena, didn't I? I included him in my Venice project after all, even if not in the same way I had originally planned.

So then, my title was gradually being fleshed out. Me was here, omnipresent, if you will. Ma and Mu were continuing. Mo had made a brief guest appearance, and Mod insinuated his way in too.

Perhaps the **&** in the title would have to be fleshed out too.

10   In My Apartment

Whenever I sit with new people, as I did the other Friday night in the rabbi's house, I always think of karma. What accident of destiny, chance, fate — the words aren't as synonymous as you would think, but don't ask me to list the differences — brought us together? Had the rabbi invited me for *Shabbat* lunch and not for Friday night, I wouldn't have met Mazal. My Mazal, my good luck. And if the rabbi had not invited Mazal, I still would have seen Ma by the Biennale but I wouldn't have known who she was.

Or consider that off-the-beaten-path walk into the calle near the synagogue, when I discovered that mezuza indentation on the right stone doorpost of an old house. Had I not taken that little curiosity stroll, I never would have met that strange man with the odd name, Mo. And how about seeing that silent pretty woman with the one eye lavender and the other chartreuse in shul on Saturday morning? Had I gone Friday night to shul and not *Shabbat* morning, I probably would not have noticed Mu at the Kiddush.

I thought these thoughts as I stood in the bathroom, looking into the mirror and waiting for Ma. I looked into that magical reflective glass not to see myself but to see myself as Mazal sees me; trying to look at myself with those big brown eyes dotted with bright orange flecks which if you stared at too long you found yourself being sucked in.

I know there was about a sixteen-year difference between us, but I didn't care. And, apparently, neither did she. She could easily have asked — but didn't — How old are you? Perhaps Roni's remark at dinner about diversity of ages, she in her mid-twenties, me in my early forties, sufficed her. Perhaps she hadn't even heard it or had tuned out.

As I looked at my image — this mystery of two faces where there was really only one has always puzzled me — I saw what I had always seen: a youthfulness that made people comment: how do you do it? (As if I did something, as if there was some kind of conscious manipulation of skin cells or the restless energy in my limbs.) You look like you're in your late twenties, is what I would hear. This youthful appearance had apparently been inherited. Both my parents looked a couple of decades younger than they were. Ditto with me. Into my early thirties I still had faint blond down on my upper cheeks that I never shaved, a kind of mark of childhood. Then one day I removed it, thinking it would grow back. It never did. And so I kissed my childhood goodbye.

Looking at myself through Mazal's eyes, I wondered what would be her assessment of me. Did she see me as a father/uncle figure, and that's why she so quickly agreed to take shelter in my apartment? Or did she regard me as a man, and hence my obligation to remember she was a modest, almost ultra-Orthodox Jewish girl?

Mazal came to my apartment with her two little suitcases. If suitcases show either wealth or poverty, and you can be sure they do, hers showed deprivation. Two sad little beaten-up bags. But there was nothing sad or beaten-up about her. She was blooming with health and in good cheer. Her opening comment was, "Tres tres gorgeous compartment."

Our chatting in the apartment was a continuation of the pleasant aura set the other day by the park bench near the Biennale. Not

Curt Leviant

even a hint of the contentious tone I had initiated at the rabbi's Friday night dinner. I didn't remind Mazal of her ridiculous desire to go to the Padua cemetery; she didn't mention my relentless criticism of Jewish superstition. She kept thanking me for offering her a place to sleep, and I thanked her for accepting my invitation with such grace and alacrity. And I restrained myself from asking her if she knew what alacrity meant.

That night Mazal slept on the sofa in the living room while I lay awake, pondering — yes, there is that intellectually weighted word again — if I should go to her, fantasizing that she was lying there awake, sizzling, wondering why I wasn't coming to her, what's wrong with him?

But I restrained myself (much easier than zipping mouth and buttoning lip). I had promised I would not forget she was a Jewish girl, almost ultra-Orthodox, very modest as she comes. At the same time I didn't forget I was ultra-heterodox, almost super-hedonox.

Don't think I didn't know I was poking fun at her when I was poking fun at her. I sure did —nastiness is not an unconscious, involuntary behavior, like breathing—being persnickety in a way she couldn't even react to. If you're sarcastic to someone and they know it, it's a two-way street. But Mazal didn't know it and, after a while, I felt a lugubrious sensation that oppressed me somewhere between my heart and my gut. A less polysyllabic and quicker way of saying it would be guilt—and I felt bad imitating her and making fun of her English.

Truth is, I wished I could speak French and mangle it the way she spoke English. At least Mazal made herself overstood. Oops, there I go again. She knew ten times as much English as I knew French. Yes, I was being nasty, I told myself, while thinking of

Hillel's famous apothegm in the Ethics of the Fathers: "Do not do to others what you don't want them to do to you."

As I lay awake, imagining various magic tricks to shorten the distance between moi and her, I began to appreciate her steadfastness, her determination, her single-mindedness, and the ethical stance behind her mission, even though I thoroughly disagreed with her means of achieving her goal. You notice I'm not using the word fanaticism.

In the middle of the night, just after I had finally fallen asleep, I sensed a presence hovering over me. I woke at once. The lone street lamp in the calle brought a half light into my room, showing me who stood there in a sleeveless green cotton nightshirt perfectly filled out.

"Pardon moi for breaking your dorm," Mazal said.

"Is okay. Can't sleep anyway."

"In realitay?"

"Oui. Tres realitay. Has something frightened you?" I asked, patting the area near my pillow. "Sit....Did you hear a noise? A mouse perhaps? An oversize squirrel. Are you afraid of something?"

"No, no, no fraid. But something non bon. Something breaken in moi body thermo-meter. Time I feel tres heat, time tres frost."

"Are you tres hot now?"

"No, tres frosting."

I felt, held, her ice cold hand.

"My God! You're freezing. So come in. Be defrosted. I have tres grand defrosting unit. I help you defrost."

She slipped in beside me, her soft "merci" almost inaudible.

Even without touching her I felt the tremor of her body. I put my arms around her, felt her shivering next to me. It was the third week in June; heat all over Venice. But Mazal was cold. I drew her close. Her body fit right into mine; her hefty breasts pressing against my chest.

"I will chase the chill, make flee the frost."

"And I say merci tres much," she said, her face next to mine. I could feel the letters of her words on my cheeks, the quiver of her lips on my skin.

"If no you, tres bon Jewish man, where would I be dorm?"

"You see, it was destined that I am your dormitory."

"Yes, but please to recall what you must to recall," Mazal said, almost into my lips.

As I ran my thumb slowly down her spine, I said, like a ventriloquist, not moving my lips:

"I will not forget what I am not supposed to forget."

"Goodly."

Then she put her finger to her cheek like she did the other day when she sat on the park bench, thinking.

"But then what I sudden feel tween moi and vous?"

I didn't have to think long and hard to answer that question.

"Is fence of protection, fence of separation, that separates vous and moi, like men and women separate sections in synagogue. Vous, one side. Moi, other."

"Oh, merci," Mazal said. And she gave out a breath of relief and kissed me on both cheeks in gratitude. "Merci pour dees dormir, pour dees welcome, pour dees respect to moi you show."

"My pleasure," I said. "You see, good fences make good neighbors."

"Is tres poetique. Dees new good neighbor fence vous have erectated, I no know if made of hard warm wood or hot brick, but it is defrost chill shivers in moi belly."

"Delighted it defrosts you. If you like, I invite you to inspect for yourself the fence I have erectated to chase away your chill shivers, and see for yourself if it is warm hard wood or a hot brick."

Mazal's eyes were closed. I removed my arms from around her back and held her face. I brought my lips to hers and kissed her. At once she pressed closer. Then, as a long moan tore through her, she rolled over on top of me, bringing her open mouth to mine. I gently kissed every tiny part of each lip. I took her upper lip between my lips, there was a faint citric taste there, and then her lower lip, which trembled between mine. And then the glissando of her Eros suddenly broke forth, that Eros that danced and slid on her skin, in her eyes, in her every movement. She began to kiss me, echoing every one of my kisses, her lips on my eyes, my nose, her tongue into each ear, kissing and licking my throat and shoulders and the nipples on my chest, sowing in me a sensation I had never felt before.

I did the same to her, savoring those grand tetons that all of us had eyed at Rabbi Roni's Friday night dinner and I alone the last couple of days. The kisses on each breast sent a scream into the air, causing a palpable fear to run through me that the polizia veneziana patrolling the Grand Canal would soon jump off their motoscafi and crash in to save whoever was screaming in pain, or painful pleasure.

From the area around my fence of protection a warmth, a heat wafted, yes, that's the correct word, wafted, floated up, rose, like a warm morning mist; it had a smell of musk, a dark perfume, and it wasn't my cloud of off-beat aromatic warmth. It was hers. Professor Umberto dei Rossi, my companion at Roni's Friday night dinner, was right again, about Mazal's sex smell.

Mazal had still not said a word. Her body was so molded into mine it seemed she wanted to invade me. Somewhere beyond her mouth sounded a little song. She clasped my back with her arms and seemed to relax. Now, with my lips on her lower lip again, just as she was removing her right hand from around my shoulder and moving it slowly down my chest, to my abdomen, she fell asleep in my embrace.

11   In the Padua Cemetery

And she woke in my embrace. After I kissed her she said:

"Today moi go to Rabbi Moses bury space, find stone of tomb of him, but moi lot fraid on spirits of dead in cementaire."

I nodded and looked into her big dark brown eyes, whose little orange yellow flecks made her eyes dance, revealing layers of black, like caves behind caves.

She lowered her eyes.

"I will take you to the Padua cemetery."

"No!" she said, surprised.

"Yes."

"Verite?"

"Oui, verite," I said.

"But you much gainst moi go."

"One thing has nothing to do with the other, lovely, sexy, passionate desire Mazal. Me against, true. But I take you anyway."

"You will?" she said. The surprised tone now turned enticing. I wondered in what school girls learn that universal melody? The tonic slant of those two words had an erotic punch and I caught a quick lingering outward flick of her tongue before she shut her mouth. And her eyes sparkled too.

"Come, let's get dressed. I looked down table-time. We have a 9:52 train to Padua. And it's a beautiful day."

"Vous ready know train o'clock?"

"Sure. Had plans to take you...But I must tell you again it will be impossible to find the Maitre's grave and tombstone. You shouldn't be disappointed."

"Moi know. Rabbi tell to moi."

"But you still want to go."

"Oui. Still. Still, Still. You see, moi find the Maitre."

I didn't say anything, but perhaps she read my mind, or at least skimmed its surface.

"If against your princip, no go. Moi think moi no fraid no more."

"That's what you're saying now, Mazal. But wait till you're in the cementaire and you're the only one there and shivers run up and down your spine and all the spirits and ghosts and dybbuks of all the dead in the cementaire compete for your attention and you start trembling with cold and frost and chills like you did last night but there's no me there to take you in to a warm bed to defrost you with a hot brick fence of protection and make you warm again."

She smiled. "Again speechify longlishly. But moi thinked you no believe in ghosts and spirits."

"I don't, Mazal. You do. Vous do. So you need voodoo protection. Are you trying to dissuade me from going?"

"No."

"Goodly....Do you know what dissuade means?"

"No."

We both laughed.

"It means, you trying to talk me out of going with you," I said. "Trying to say to me, stay home. I go moiself. Do you want me to go with you?"

"Oui," Mazal cried out. "Double oui. Oui, oui, oui."

Although it was only one word, I saw an entire vocabulary there behind her eyes. Oh, there were loads of words unsaid behind her eyes.

"Fine. I like that oui. That means *we* go to cementaire together."

And she was also so pleased when I told her that in times of trouble, Jews had a tradition of running to the cemetery, crying at tombstones, figuring if the living could not help, perhaps the dead might.

"Bon," Mazal said. "So you see? Moi non so different from other juifs. And I so so glad you go and come with moi. Yes. Verite. Muchly. But moi still puzzle pour...how you word say when one thing you do and say another?"

"Contradiction."

"You full contradiction."

"At least I'm not full of bad linen."

"You laughy man."

"But, yes, I am full of contradictions. Men are wrapped in contradictions. As a cunning linguist, I am now working on a new type of dictionary. It's called a contradictionary. It will list words that are opposite of what they mean. Here's an example of how people are full of contradictions. Even famous good men are full of them. The first Prime Minister of Israel, David Ben Gurion, epitomized an amazing contradiction during World War Two, when the British issued the infamous White Paper that restricted the number of Jews allowed to enter Palestine. Ben Gurion said, We will fight the British on this as if there is no war, and we will fight with the British against the Germans as though there is no White Paper. In other words, going back to vous and moi, I can be skeptical about your mission and still enjoy being with you as you try to accomplish it... And this is the first citation in my contradictionary...Overstand?"

"No," Mazal said and burst into a merry, provocative laugh.

"You speechify overly and longingly like on Friday night at rabbin's home."

"And, anyway, I want to help you find this non-existent grave. I love contradictions and oxymorons."

Out of one of her two little battered suitcases she took out a pair of short shorts. In honor of the visit to the Jewish cementaire she put on a demure, long-sleeved white blouse. I hadn't paid attention to her legs. But now I looked at them, a bit on the chubby side, not sleek or slim; but then again, as I said, Ma was only about five-three — short, busty, pretty girls are the best — and after her face, her eyes, and her U.S. national park mountain range, the Grand Tetons (I cite them for readers of *Me, Mo, Mu, Ma & Mod* in translation), who looked at legs?

Mazal regarded my neat slacks and white shirt and asked, "Why you up-dressed?"

"In honor of cemetery, holy place, this is the way I dress."

"Tres goodly," Mazal said. "You have overcovering for head, like on Friday night dinner?"

"Of course. I bring my *kippa*, in honor of cementaire," and I showed her my yarmulke.

On the vaporetto to the train station we sat in the front and pretended our private boat was sailing through the Grand Canal, showing us the palazzos gliding by on the left and on the right.

"Moi still puzzle," Mazal said, frowning, "why you go to buryplace with moi if nay believe Maitre power."

"Okay, let me put it this way, Mazal of the Puzzles. If a hypochondriac..." I pronounced it the European way, "who is perfectly healthy wants to visit a doctor, you still take him as an act of personal kindness."

But she misunderstood me, for she said, "Why hippo need doctor?"

"Sick. Mal de tete."

When the vaporetto stopped at the train station Mazal looked at me. She still couldn't understand my motive.

"You fine Jewish man. Still is question. If vous against visit cementaire, why you go?"

If one can create a tone that combines a bit of contentiousness with flirtation Mazal had the recipe.

"I'm against it for vous, not for moi. But what's more important, I don't want you to go alone to the cemetery. I am your fence of protection."

Mazal took a step closer to me, brought her face close to mine. There was a lovely good humor in her eyes, a warmth, a memory of recognition as she blazed her orange-dotted big brown-eyed glance into mine: "Like fence of protection you erectate in mid night pour defrost moi."

"Even bigger fence."

Mazal smiled a happy smile.

"Bon. Moi fraid way ago."

On the broad steps of the terminal, Mazal said,"Moi…" and stopped. She rubbed her thumb on two fingers, "... soon jogging out of euro."

"Worry not. When I said, I take you, I meant really take you. Pay for your trip."

At the ticket booth I bought two first-class tickets.

"Prima class?" Mazal said. "Too tres euro. Why prima?"

"Because you're prima, that's why," I said and kissed her ear. She looked about, cheeks flushed, probably hoping that no one from the community had witnessed this.

In the car she admired the first-class accouterments. For a while we rode in silence. With my arm around her, she nestled her head on my shoulder. Then, suddenly, she sat up and repeated my dream that I had told her on the park bench the other day.

"See? You dream prophetish. Like Yosef in Bible. We ride on vaporetto. And now on train. But elevator is miss."

The smile she gave sent messages exploding like fireworks in many directions. Oh, those lascivious *Decameron* rhyming words that this almost ultra-Orthodox sex bombshell inspired in me.

"Elevator not missing. You will find elevator too."

"Moi so verité tres satisfait vous come with moi." She threw her arms around my neck and kissed my lips with fervor. And during that kiss she found my hand and pressed it to her heart.

"I hope to satisfait you again. Content to come with you. Mazal, you delicious, like fresh baguette."

And I meant it. She was delicious. Her mouth, her lips, her face, the entirety of her.

"And during that dinner in Roni's house, although you looked totally delicious then, I never dreamt you would put your lips on mine. But I admit I thought of putting my hands on you, all over you."

"After Friday night longish speechify moi no dream in moi wild test dream vous come with moi in cementaire."

Yes, true, I contradicted myself — a candidate for my contra-dictionary — now joining a mission I had argued against loudly and fervently. I thought of this as we both watched the swiftly moving countryside. I wanted to penetrate the mystery of her going to this long-dead rabbi. What would this superstition-laden trip accomplish? Speaking to the dead was entirely foreign to Jewish principles, yet accepted by the common folk as Jewish practice.

Would this encounter bring her honor in her congregation back in the poor suburb of Paris? I was keen on entering her gestalt, which is not a synonym for a woman's most elemental entry point.

A bit of research showed me that Rabbi Moses was a famous early eighteenth century kabbalist of Spanish descent much favored by the superstitious-prone North African Jews. He had assured his followers, to whom he dispensed blessings left and right, like a Pope on a pilgrimage, that even after his death anyone who visited his grave would be blessed with good fortune and a boost, like an injection of Vitamin B-12, of elevated spirituality. He was also an advocate for communal peace and protected those falsely accused. For Mazal it would be as if she had come with an empty sack and would now carry back home a cartful of beneficence.

During the train ride I reflected upon Mazal's mission. She had already shown me that she had lots of passion for religion. Only someone with such passion would travel hundreds of miles to a different country and spend a lot of money to visit the grave of a famous long-dead rabbi to ask him to intervene in a communal quarrel. Or if not to overtly ask him, but just to be in the presence of his tombstone, as if that stone had some magical or ameliorative power, that too is an act of religious passion.

Or pagan passion.

Yes, Judaism has it too. Even in the Torah. Don't think that pagan elements haven't seeped into what is touted as pure monotheism. Remember that brass, or brazen, snake—in Hebrew the two words, **nekhash ha-nekhoshet,** have the same root and are a superb pun or word-play—that Moses held up and which stopped the plague? Not God, not Moses, but the pagan brazen snake. But no religious Jew wants to believe that. They buy the rabbinic explanation, a serpentine cover-up, that the Israelites looked up —

up to God, that is, and not at the snake made of brass.

Only pagans believe in magical creatures made of metal or stone. And everyone agrees that religious and physical passion are linked, like the left hand and the right. One is an outlet for the other, and both are tied to the same source. Somerset Maugham had his finger on that pulse in his story about the up-tight, super-religious minister/missionary and the woman he meets somewhere in a South Sea island. I think the story is called "Rain". The ancients grasped this link and transformed it into sacred ritual: the holy whore, the temple sex priestess. No wonder the Hebrew root for holiness, **k-d-sh**, is embedded in the Hebrew word for prostitute, *kedesha*.

Mazal's split personality was revealed at once at the Friday night dinner as soon as she entered with her white blouse open at the top two buttons. And that's what that Italian professor, Umberto dei Rossi, said when I met him a day later near the train station. He said that Mazal could snap either way in a minute.

At the gate of the cemetery I hesitated. The place was deserted; not a soul around.

"You no enter?" Mazal asked. "Because you kohen?"

"Why you ask?"

"Because in Judaisme kohen forhibbited to sit feet in cementaire, except for closet relative."

"Forhibbited?"

"You know, probidden. No no." She waved her index finger back and forth. "Dispermitted. Interdit."

"Aha! And what is closet relative? I only keep my grandma in my closet. No one else."

Mazal laughed. "No no no. You not overstand moi." And to

demonstrate she hugged herself and rocked her breasts. "Closet relative...mama, papa, sisteur, brodeur."

"Ah. Oh. Now I see. You mean closest relatives."

"Oui. Now you overstand moi."

"No no. I not a kohen."

"Then why you stand here by gate? Moi thought you go in cementaire with moi. You now too pullet, too hen, to enter bury place of dead?"

"You right. I too rooster, too capon, to set foot here. It is too creepy, this old cemetery. Overgrown with weeds. Not a soul around. I told you I would take to you to Padua cemetery but I didn't say I would go through, enter, go in, set foot therein."

Mazal looked heartbroken, near tears. "Moi thought you go all way with moi." She stretched out her hand to me. "No be fraid. Moi take you."

And in I went.

"Is beautiful cementaire," Mazal said, soon as she set foot in this picturesque place.

I had seen a cemetery like this only once, in a Yiddish film, *The Dybbuk*, made in Poland just before the war. For a crucial scene, the director had chosen one of the old cemeteries outside of Warsaw, one just like this, where the tombstones were bent, half sunken, and stone slabs stuck out in all directions, without any plan or symmetry. Here the weeds grew high and were bent over too, mimicking the stones. Likely no one had set foot in here in years. Some tombstones were so old the inscribed letters were faded. Rabbi Moses had indeed been buried here but no trace of his grave remained. But this hadn't dissuaded Mazal, for she took stock in luck, amulets, folk belief — a world that negates facts, pooh-poohs science and history. It thrives in a sphere where the letters of the Hebrew alphabet are read as numbers and send out esoteric messages that cause followers to gasp in wonder and delight at the secrets revealed to them. Called *gematria,* from the Greek word *geometria,* this playful Hebrew numbers game is taken by many to be a bona fide branch of Biblical commentary.

For Mazal dreamworld was more potent than fact.

So how was she different from me, argued my other self, who preferred speculation to fact and saw the truth of fiction over the truth of fact?

Mazal insisted she would find the Maitre of Padua. And she was so flattered, flirtatious too, when I told her I'd go with her. How could I not take her, when she attracted me in Roni's apartment, when I dreamed of her, when she had spent the night with me? That little charmer's eyes drew me; her religiosity with its taint and taste of spice; her take-me body.

In this old Jewish graveyard the ground was uneven. One had to proceed step by step. Although I wanted to lead the way, Mazal insisted on going first. I think she wanted to spot Rabbi Moses's tombstone before me.

We'll never find it, I thought.

But this twenty-first century witch read my mind.

"We will find," she said. "Moi look with moi eyes full of care."

We had hardly gone three strides when she tripped on a stone and fell forward with a little cry. I sprang forward to try to catch her, but luckily, she caught hold of a tombstone that broke her fall.

"Okay, that's it," I said. "Now we hold hands. Go together."

I led the way and we walked along the narrow bumpy twisting path that we ourselves created for there was no straight walkway here. As we moved slowly we looked at the inscription on each stone. We could not walk side by side. My left hand was stretched out behind me and her left hand grasped mine and that's how we made our way slowly. Our hands parted only when we stopped to look at one old tombstone. It dated back more than three hundred years. I stood in awe for a moment, impressed by its antiquity.

But Mazal had no patience for sentiment. Hopeful, she urged me on.

When we came to the fence, we turned and went back a different way.

Suddenly, I heard her cry out, "Attention! I see!"

So she found it after all, went through my mind.

"The rabbin you say buried in Venice. His here."

"What? You mean Rabbi Leone da Modena?"

Mazal pointed to the old tombstone.

"Non Venice. Here. Read. Modena."

I looked, then sighed. "No, Mazal. That's Medina, another common name, like the word in Hebrew for 'country'. And, look, his first name is Yosef, not Leone, or, in Hebrew, Aryeh."

Mazal lowered her head, downcast. I thought she was going to cry.

"I am so apologize."

I held her. "That's all right, Mazal. It was so nice of you to remember and think of me. Easy mistake. The letters and sound almost so same."

I held Mazal, but Modena held me too. This, the Jewish cementaire, among the canopy of tombstones, would be a good place to bring in Modena to erect a canopy for us, to cement our relationship. I'm sure he'd love to be included. And if a canopy, we would need a witness. Rabbi Roni was out, but I knew another man in Venice who I'd like to get to know better—Mo.

Mo would fit in to Me, Mo, Ma & Mod, but that leaves out Mu. But then a brilliant idea struck me. Maybe like Abraham with Sarah and Hagar, and Jacob with Rachel and Leah, I could have Ma *and* Mu. So now my title, *Me, Mo, Mu, Ma & Mod* is complete again.

Thinking of Modena made him come to me, as if in a waking dream, a vision, a sighting halfway between waking and sleep. Not unexpected if you're walking one bright warm sunny day in a deserted cementaire and if you have the mazal, the good fortune, of spending the morning with a pious, modest, sex-loving Mazal.

"You!" I exclaimed as I saw Modena before me.

Did Mazal see him too?

Probably not, otherwise she would have screamed.

"Don't forget it's me that got you a free sailing on this Venice Fellowship," Mod said with restrained anger, "because you told the committee you plan to write about me…"

"But," I interrupted Modena, "they also wrote to me that I'm not bound to my proposal."

"Still, bear in mind, it's because of me you're here. I've provided you with the beneficent winds that filled your fellowship's sails. If not for me, you wouldn't have met Mu and Ma…"

"How do you know Mu and Ma?"

"I know everything."

He looked at me, Mod did, this short and natty man, with a wise look.

"And then not only did you drop me, you assumed I'm buried in Padua."

"Dead wrong, Mod. I assumed no such thing. It was Ma's error."

"No. It's yours, for you created Mazal."

"In that case," was my clever riposte, "I also created you."

That silenced him.

"But it will please you, Signor Rabbino Modena that, in fact, I'm going to include this very scene here at the cementaire with you… I haven't forgotten you at all. You are constantly in my mind."

With that last word uttered Modena vanished. Done my day vision with Mod.

I shook my head as though to clear the cobwebs, remembering that Mazal was with me.

I turned to her and said:

"Remember what you said at Roni's dinner about mazal, constellation, and what my reaction was?"

"Oui. Certainment. And moi not like you for that. No, no, not you personal, but you words."

"But you will be happy to know, now I believe in constellations. Mazal, singular, and mazalot, plural."

"Is true? Verite, verite?"

"Oui. *You* are my mazal. My constellation."

"That is tres nice." Again she pronounced it like the French resort city.

"Remember, in rabbi's house Friday night dinner, you quote ibn Ezra, the mazal that has power over certain places? Yes, now I know it is true. Now I believe it."

Mazal put her hands on her hips and looked at me with surprise.

"Non! You convertize? So rapidement?"

"Mais oui. You, Mazal, have power over me."

She looked up at me. In the orange dots of her eyes I saw tiny magnets pulling me. I pressed my right palm to her face, lifted it

Curt Leviant

slightly.

She said, Oh. A long Oh that started high and ended low. I pressed, touched, her shoulder. The top of her breast. The muscle of her arm. Touch, press, move. Each time the same Oh of joy, of longer and deeper timbre.

Then, like Goethe — while in the embrace of his mistress, he would experiment with syllabic beats by tapping his fingers on her back — I experimented too. I switched hands and continued with my magical left, the one imprinted with Mu's *Shabbat*. The Ohs came quicker, more breathy, extending into excited Ahs that ended with a quivering vibrato because of the three letters of *Shabbat* שבת pressing on her skin. Proving my point that religion and sex were intersected in the very makeup of our bodies.

I bent forward and kissed her lips, first the lower, then the upper one.

"When last time you sweeped your tooths?"

"You mean brushed? For my Bar Mitzva. Why? Does it taste bad?"

"No no. Is delicious. When boys sweep tooth I taste teeth-taste. Ek!"

"Nah. I don't use toothpaste. Ek, is right. So my mouth taste good?"

"Tres sexy. Real. Taste like chemical sex comes up from down below."

"So taste again."

"Mmm," she said. "You only sweep special occasion?"

"Mais oui. Bar Mitzva. Wedding."

"No," she moaned. "No," she cried out in shock. "You wedded? Moi commit adulthood with you?"

"No worry. No wedded no more. One kiss after wedding,

wife tastes ek pastetooth and says me, Au revoir...Now me no sweep tooth no more."

Mazal waved her hand at me. "Me no credible one word you say, you laughy man." And she kissed me again.

I looked into her eyes and smiled. I made a kissing motion with my lips. Again I pressed my hands to her cheeks. At once an electric shock went through her, like the shock that I felt when mute Gila, Mu with the two differently-colored eyes, inscribed the three Hebrew letters of *Shabbat* on my palm. Mazal threw her arms quickly around me and, with a long, musical, enchanting "ah", she entwined her tongue into mine, then pressed my face down to her breast. While I quickly unbuttoned her blouse, she brought hands to the back of her bra.

It took her a while to unhook it. She asked me to help. Most bras have one or two clasps; hers had three. It took four hands to do the undoing. When we finally undid it she threw the bra over one of the tilted tombstones. It tilted even more. Now tetons are usually compared to melons. But hers, large, weighty, firm, with a neat oval slope, put all melons to shame. And the nipples and the aureoles around them were brass hued, as though they'd come from a different planet.

"Incredible," I said. "What a beautiful color. The nipples. The aureoles. Like burnished brass. Never seen anything like that." I buttoned my lip re the brass serpent. But worshiper paganly any-way.

"Moi upwoke one day ago two years and such it were."

"Were you worried? Did you see a doctor?"

"Oui. I see top nosh doctor. Very full of care. He spend long clock examine all over. No rush, no quick one two three bye-bye. Fifteen twenty minute. On each one. He exam real goodly. With this arm. That arm. Two hands. Touch. Hold. Squeege."

"Did he kiss them?"

Mazal laughed. "Non. He non verpert like you. Find no wrong. Moi tres healthy."

"Yes. Bursting with health, and stunning too."

She held them up with two hands toward me like an offering

"You sure two hands are enough?"

"Non. Better four hand."

"Amazing."

"Moi knowing," she said. And then she added something touching: "All peoples has something special. Per moi, this. Moi grand tetons."

"And for moi, Mazal, you are special. All of Mazal. Not just this."

"Tleast peoples know moi a girl."

"One girl? You're three and three-quarters girl plus five thousand frequent flier miles."

And then I kissed those two beautiful, blue-veined breasts, lifted those heavy grand tetons and kissed the brass-colored nipples as she sang out vowels I had never heard before. Hawaiian has twelve; Fijian eighteen. I counted thirty-six of Mazal's before I lost track.

"Are you restless in excitation of yearning?" I said.

She smiled, pleased that I remembered her phrase of Friday night.

"Oui. Moi joy moiself with you. Moi have tres good clock with you."

"And do I recall you are a Jewish girl?"

"Oui. You possess grand recall. You froget no thing," Mazal said, her eyes shining.

"And I recall also you are ultra-Orthodox."

"Now you no recall goodly." A wise look overspread her face. "You froget moi say, *almost* ultra-Orthodox."

I brought her down to the soft earth.

"Off. Off," she commanded, pulling at my clothes.

I offed while kissing her. It took some acrobatics, working with two, three, four hands and one leg, but I did it. I touched the left edge of one breast with the tips of my fingers while the soft part of my arm below the elbow was at the other edge, so wide was her teton. I ran one finger between her fingers, spread open the fingers, and kissed the empty four spaces. She loved it. She wriggled and twisted. She couldn't take it. This had never happened to her before.

The earth was warm, the sun shone, the grass was dry. Between the bent and silent tombstones we found a nice spot and stretched out on the grass. Between the bent and silent tombstones that almost formed a canopy over us.

I imagined her saying, "Please non get moi prey-nyan."

"I once read in a holy book," I assured her, "that one can never get pregnant in a holy place."

"Please don't up knock me," she continued, making the "k" hard, so it came out like this:

"Don't up ke-nock me."

"Is conundrum necessaire?" I asked.

Her eyes were closed. She loved to close her eyes. She shook her head.

Oh my, thinks I. Is this little sexpot on the pill? Or does she already have a diaphragm in place? Perhaps she has a little vial of morning-after pills.

Without opening her eyes Mazal said, "Moi near end moi

lunicycle. Soon moi comma come."

"Comma?" Again a riddled word dance.

She looked quite fetching smiling with her eyes closed.

"Excuse moi. Un error. Non comma. Soon arrive moi semi-colon. So tres bien sans condumdrum."

At once I thought of that three-dimensional semi-colon that I had seen in the synagogue, lifting up off the printed page of the Siddur. I had puzzled over that. But now I knew why I saw a semi-colon, which is comprised of a comma and period. It was an adumbration, like in any good fiction, a foretelling of an event. Had I asked the rising semi-colon, Why are you here? — just as I had asked Mo why he was here in Venice soon as I entered the Ghetto— maybe I would have received an answer. The same ambiguous one that Mo had given me.

That semi-colon appeared to give me a hint of things to come. The two punctuation points were not related. A period wasn't a comma, and a comma wasn't a period. They had distinctly different roles. But combining the two showed that on occasion they could be joined and give meaning to each other. Now Mazal's remark made sense. For her the comma was a period.

The stones, old and older, the crooked and the slant, moved up and down, nodding their heads at us, reflecting the sun's rays onto Mazal's warm, warming, body. She trembled; she shook; she vibrated like a plucked string, a phenomenon totally new for me. Her vibrating cast me into Venus.

"Oh God," she sang. "Oh God. Oh God, Mon Dieu" she cried. "Moi love it. Moi love it. Moi love it. Oh God, mon Dieu, mon Dieu, Oh, how moi love love love it. Your fence de protection you erectated."

I had never heard sounds like that before. Low pitched groans, high pitched squeals, cries of joy in the middle register. I thought she would wake the dead. Mazal was singing harmony with herself, quaking, shaking, full of tremors as she sang the song of her delight, not in English but in French, and I translate as best I can that music of delirium ecstasy.

"Are you fou, crazy, for it?"

"*Fou.* Crazy. Tres tres fou. Is best. Is nothing bester in tout le monde, Msieur Speechify. You make moi arrivey again et again."

"How many arrivey?"

"Moi stop count. Moi can't count so altitude."

"Is this your preferred position?"

"What mean preferred?"

"You like it this way?"

"Oui."

"Or another way?"

"All ways."

"Remember, Mazal, you said, I wish angel give me divine massage. And I told you maybe surely time will come. Well, isn't, wasn't, this a divine massage?"

"Oui. From sky."

"You mean heaven."

"Oui. From heaven. You give bon massage from heaven. Verite. You tres tres bon therapiste physicalement."

I hugged her, kissed her again. Her lips, cheeks, nose, eyes.

"Mazal, you're delightful. There's no one like you."

"Why you say no one like moi. Everyone like moi."

"No, you no overstand. I mean to say you are special. Unique. There is no one like you. No one similar to you."

Tears came to her eyes. "And moi no find Rabbi Moses."

"But you found the Maitre of Padua."

"Where?"

"Remember, you said, I find the Maitre."

"Oui."

"Well, you found him. And the missing elevator too."

"Ou est le Maitre?"

"Here. Right next to you, Le Maitre, c'est moi."

She smiled a blissful smile. "Perhaps you have right."

"You know why I say that? Because my Hebrew name is Moses. Yes, it is. Really. Verite. So when you go back home, tell them you had a mystic union with Reb Moses in the cementaire and now you bring back home your mission of peace."

"Bon. Tres bon."

"And you can tell that to the rabbi's wife also."

Mazal narrowed her glance at me.

"How you know about rabbi wife?"

"Moses, c'est moi, knows everything. So when you go back to Paris, tell them your mission was successful. You found le Maitre. You found Moses. And I also fulfilled your wish. You said, I wish you come with me. And I did. I came with you. You came with me. We came together in the cementaire."

It was so beautifully quiet here. Not even a bird sang here. The only sounds came from the chitter of cicadas.

We lay there naked, holding each other in tranquility on this warm summer afternoon, enjoying life amid the old granite tombstones that testified to rest in peace. But then I felt an awkward feeling, as though something were rubbing me the wrong way. The sensation of bliss was slipping away, a bliss too good to be true, for as I pressed Mazal closer to me, my palms on her back, I felt a pulsing in my palm and hoped she didn't feel it. I dared not ask. Since Mazal was silent, I held my peace too.

But I felt there were three of us here.

Then, suddenly, oh my God, were those footfalls I was hearing — I held Mazal tight — or was it my imagination? Oh no, Gila's coming after me, my artiste de tootoo, as Mazal put it.

"What is?" she said.

"Nothing. I think I heard footsteps... Can it be the rabbi's?" Even though I knew it wasn't he.

Now she held me tight.

"Maybe he come to critique moi."

For your affairs with the rabbis, both of them, I thought a nasty thought, then edited it out. But there was no one; it was all in my imagination.

The Padua cemetery was dead still.

Nevertheless, as if reading my mind, she volunteered:

"The Venezia rabbi unfilled jug. Materialist..."

On the contrary, I thought. Materialists do not go into the rabbinate.

"But you," she looked at me. "You a think person. Even moi no agree with you, you thinking and you find favor in balls of moi eyes."

We sat up. I hugged her again, ran my finger over her cheek.

"Moi loving touch. Soon as man touch moi, moi am Danish."

I controlled my laughter. "I think you want to say finish."

"Oui," and she laughed. "Moi mix moi nationalitay. Moi am finish soon as man touch moi. Caput. Moi into hell sinki."

The orange yellow glittered in her eyes, but I couldn't tell if the joke was purposeful or a sweet accident.

Of course, Mazal wouldn't have, couldn't have, known a

thing about this, but the proximity of death, the fusion of sex, death and God that the English poet, John Donne, had celebrated so succinctly and emblematically in his verses, dying for love, dying in love, expiring in love, pouring out your soul in love, pouring out your soul in prayer, the orgasm of love and death. All this was right up his alley. Here, here, here, among and under the Padua tombstones, we had it too.

And Mazal also echoed this point beautifully with her repeated orgasmic cry of Oh God, mon Dieu, her own version of Donne's verses, showing how divine was this earthly delight.

Meanwhile, metaphysics aside, we leaned against a tombstone, relaxed and happy, not even hungry or thirsty. We had brought nothing with us.

"Oui," she said aloud, breaking the somnolent silence, "Moi tres tres love touch."

"Don't I know it," I said.

"Soon as man touch moi, moi almost ultra-Orthodox fly out fenetre and moi become ultra-Danish, ultra-Swede, ultra-Finnish."

"Me too," I said.

"Quoi?" She backed away from me. "Soon as man touch you? You, you also on other side? Play both side?"

"Don't worry." And I clasped her grand tetons. "I play one side of fence only. When I said, Me too, I mean to say soon as woman touches me I'm Danish too."

She looked thoughtful for a moment, then added:

"Moi plummet in love tres rapidement. A guy put arm surround moi, bim bam, moi loco *fou* for him."

"For me too?" I asked Mazal.

She smiled, opened wide her eyes. Tried to make her smile

say, But not you, mon Msieur Speechify.

"Maybe it's not me. It's my touch." And I moved my middle finger slowly up her arm from her wrist to her shoulder. A little rill of shivers moved through her like a breeze. I remembered the scenario I had created for myself regarding Mazal. That the Paris rabbi's wife had made an indirect accusation against her. Which prompted this entire mission to Padua. And as it turned out, I was absolutely right.

"I think it's rabbis you are *fou* for, Mazal. Rabbi Moses. Maybe the rabbi in Paris too. And Venice."

"Non. Not Roni. But verite, moi like holy men. They make moi spirit tres high excited."

First your spirit, then you, runs through my mind.

"Up up up like elevator." She cast a knowing glance at me. "Warm moi religionosity in restless yearning."

Restless yearning? That phrase she must have gotten from some romantic potboiler.

"It's so good you're so attractive and sexy and religious and desirable, mon tres jolie, charmant Mazal."

"But Friday at rabbi's house you verite angry with moi."

"Can you imagine how angry I would have been if you were not so pretty?"

"And what if moi ugly?"

"Then I would have been even more hard on you....*Be'emet*." I added in Hebrew: honestly.

"Where you learn ebreu?"

"From my mama's milk. Moi mama and papa know ebreu and I inherit. Just like a bebe does not go to universite to learn to suck milk from mama's tetons, so I learned my ebreu by going to breast....like this...."

She squealed as I started nuzzling.

"Is good?" I asked.

"Tres excellent."

"See? This is way I learned ... now the other one."

To which I brought my tongue and held it there until the nipple stiffened. Now it looked like a brightly polished brass button. Then I affixed my lips and stayed a while.

"You....ah....oh....learn tres much. You eggs sellent student."

"Vraiment. Maintenant, je parle français sans problème."

"Quoi!"

"Mais oui. You see, just as I learned ebreu from my mammy's teton, I learn francais from you."

"Is miracleuse."

"Now I go back for second semester French. From such grand tetons my tongue can learn seventy tongues in a snap... Tell me, you have such a grand basket to hold such a grand teton." I pointed to her bra. "What size is this? Forty-two DDD."

She didn't understand. Obviously, the French had a different size system.

"No size," she said. "Pour moi, by kilo." And she lifted one. "One kilo. To brassiere shop moi say, Un soutien-gorge, un kilo, pour each side and other."

Now we found another stretch of grass between the tombstones. While I expanded my French, Mazal showed off her treasury of vowels.

"Oh...ah...uh...ay...we...."

"Mazal, you sing so beautifully....You like music?"

"Oui."

"Which instruments?"

"Violon and piano....When big violonist, Jascha Perlman,

come in Paris, moi come. And every time big penist, froget his name, come in Paris, moi come many time."

"That's why you healthy girl. Most people don't know whether they're coming or going. But you sure know the difference."

She started putting on her blouse. Had she forgotten about her restraint system? Now she looked even sexier than before with her breasts filling out the blouse naturally.

Then she lifted her blouse again.

"Desire you plus education en francais pour augmenter le vocabulaire?"

Does verbal charm have an erotic pull? Hers sure did. Sitting next to Mazal and listening to her, her eyes closed in bliss, I felt my protective fence stirring again with desire. So since she was soon expecting her lunar comma, semi-colon, or any other punctuation point, I put in my bid for Advanced French.

In my arrogance, in my — yes, I admit, for I only tell the truth here in this real tale — conceit, insufferable is an adjective usually connected with that word, I thought to myself that upstairs Mazal was a locus, a center of feelings, sensations, emotions, with a vocal range that top notch sopranos rarely achieve; but her downstairs was a veritable cerebrum, smart, imaginative, brimming with know-how.

"Mazal, tell me, did you ever do this in a cemetery before?"

"Non in this," she replied at once.

A swirl of colors encompassed me. Green, mixed with scarlet, yellow, ultramarine. Who says jealousy is only green? First it's an entire palette; then a dark blue feeling jabs you and makes you sink.

That she did not smile, the vixen, annoyed me. At least she should have smiled to tell me she was joking. But where else did she have the opportunity? At the Jewish cemetery on the Lido? And with whom? Or in Paris? Impossible. Surely, she was joking. Teasing me.

I brought her close, assumed a serious mien and stared into her eyes. No special reaction. I let it pass. No use making a fuss about such nonsense. And then, just as my heart registered another little downturn of depression and jealousy, she tapped my nose with her forefinger and laughed.

"Moi make a grand laugh." And then added, "You tres gooder then any rabbi."

But I didn't know if she meant the one in Venice, the one in Paris, or the one here, whom she hadn't found.

I looked up at the sun. Here, it seemed to me, time had stood still. But the sun had moved. How many hours had we spent here in this quiet paradise? Then Mazal said:

"We come here. Now we go." She started putting on her clothes.

As I dressed I felt a pulsing and for a moment I hallucinated and saw before me Gila's pretty face, as I had seen it in the synagogue behind the latticework. Her lavender eye, her chartreuse eye, both were expressionless, as if someone had taken a passport photo of her. It would be too much to say that in my quick vision of her Mu said something to me. But the throbbing of the three letters on my palm, pulsing like a pulse with a pulse's rhythm, spelled out Me, Me, Me. You're forgetting me. And she was right. I had forgotten her.

Just as we were leaving the cementaire, Mod came back for a return appearance.

Again Mazal was totally unaware of our conversation.

"What? Back again. I don't know who's manipulating whom?

You me, or me you."

"You mean," Modena said, "Me Mod, or Mod Me."

I didn't answer. I just smiled. So did Mod.

Then he added, "Mod the Manipulator."

But there was a slight uptick in his voice, as though a question. So I didn't know if his words were more assent or denial.

On the Padua train station platform my entire argument for not visiting the cemetery returned. I tried to reign in my passion; I tried to button my lip, but I was unsuccessful.

"Mazal, you recall in Roni's house we argued about superstition?"

"Oui. And moi recall that in pray book for new luna, when we make bless for new luna, we Sephardim say a bless for new luna with words *siman tov*."

"You see? I told you the Sephardim are full of superstitions." I said it gently; tried to smile. "I told you *siman tov* shows belief in power of constellations. Not in God."

Mazal smiled too. But in her smile there seemed to a little glimmer of victory. "After Friday night moi look in Ashkenaz pray book. You no know the pray for new luna. Tell! You pray the pray called *Kiddush Levana* before new luna com?"

"Never. You right. I know about it but I don't say it. Ever."

"Ashkenazim, you Jews from Europa, also say *siman tov*. And jump three time up to new luna."

"They do? That's awful. Terrible. Pagan. That's a remnant of moon worship. You know why they do that? They do that because primitive people thought that when the moon disappeared at the end of the month that's that. No more moon. Goodbye light by night. Goodbye moon. And when it came back they literally jumped for joy... I tell you, Mazal, you and me, we have to found a new Jewish religion, stripped of all pagan elements. And you're going to be my new mezuza, which I will kiss right now."

"Moi go to Paris happy." And she placed her hand on her delectable heart.

"Will you come back to Venice?"

"You want moi to come?"

"Of course."

"Moi write you."

On the train, thinking over these past few hours, I muttered almost unconsciously:

"That's it."

"What is?"

"For that foundation, I was supposed to write something about Venice. So I chose an interesting rabbi who lived here, Leone da Modena. But I decided not to focus on him. Compared to you he's boring. Since you're much more interesting, much of my focus will be on you."

"Moi? You make laughy."

"No, Mazal, I'm not joking. You're going to be the heroine of my story."

No need to tell her that as each day passed I felt more and more removed from that Modena project. Day by day Mod was drifting further away from me, as if he were on a little boat getting smaller and smaller. Even though he accented he was responsible for my ship coming to shore. For my meeting Ma and Mu. Maybe because of Mod I also met Mo. Even with mute Gila in the mix,

Modena was no longer a subject that ignited my passion. And so, after meeting Gila and Mazal, I decided not to write fiction, but the truth. What I mean is, I'll include Modena, but he won't play a leading role.

For a while I still had a slight hope I could bring in some material about Mod and weave it into fiction. But now I was sure. No fiction about him. Just true events. Like meeting him in the cementaire. In any case, truth, even if stretched a bit, is more alluring, more exciting, more delicious than fiction....

You know what? Mod has hexed me so much he has fuzzed the borders between those two opposite poles.

"Yes, absolutely, Mazal. I am going to write about you."

"Merci. Merci. Moi am honor to will be in romance. Moi love romanian scribbleur. You desire moi writetype romance you scribble?"

"Well, I certainly don't want you to wrongtype it. Maybe if it's finished and you come back to Venice you will writetype it for me. Do you know how to type?"

"Non. For you moi study writetypism. Can moi will be your secretaire?"

"I am honored you would desire to study typism for me. But I must tell you I don't trust secretaries. I handwrite everything, have poor calligraphy..."

"Calligraphy, what is?"

"Fancy word for handwriting. My right hand handwriting looks like a lefty's slanty scrawl. First I write by hand, then I type it up myself. Then correct. Then type again, without secretaire. It's because once I had an awful experience with a secretary who typed for me. She forgot, neglected — maybe even purposely edited out — a crucial negative, the word 'not', from a sentence, which turned the entire plot upside down. It introduced an unintended and widely praised ambiguity to my story. The story, then, with its interesting turn, was not mine but hers. That annoyed me even more. It also bothered me that another set of fingers, governed by a different will, could of its own volition play, and play havoc, with my words."

Mazal looked disappointed and pouted—she probably didn't understand one word I said—but as soon as I kissed her hand her mood changed.

"You speechify again tres tres longishly pour shortly question and moi small overstand speechification."

"You have right. I am tres wordy. But I know everything."

Wait. That sentence sounds familiar. Yes, Mod just said it to me in my daydream.

Then she cocked her head, looked at me, and said with a flirtatious tone in her voice:

"You really knowing everything?"

"Yes. I know everything. I am a golem."

I don't think she knew what a golem was. But I wasn't going to get into that topic now.

Afterchapter 11   Gila and Mazal, Compared

That enticing little vixen, Mazal, played her role — no, sorry, that isn't right. That would be malignation, and I'm totally against malignation, even though I don't know exactly what that word means. Mazal didn't play a role. She wasn't enticing in the classical sense, luring with practiced wiles, with knowledge aforethought, using premeditated actions, a set of womanly plans, to seduce a guy. If a girl has that, you can see that foxiness in her eyes, and I didn't see it in Mazal's. And she wasn't a vixen either. I just liked the phrase "enticing little vixen"; including it sounds writerly.

With Mazal it was all natural, even innocent, I'd say, and we conversed with ease. There wasn't the slightest tone of seduction in the melody of her voice nor in the words she uttered. One path to seduction is for the girl to ask the guy, with lure in her voice and glitter in her wide-open eyes (never mind the eyelashes fluttering, that's pulp fiction bull pillowcase), all about himself. She never did. She never asked or talked about me. For her I was on a kind of one-dimensional time zone; maybe even less than that. Neither my past nor my future interested her. She never asked where I had grown up and where I had studied. And she never inquired why I was in Venice and what I was doing here. It was I who told her.

Regarding herself, however, she operated in all three tenses. Her actions in the present lassoed in both the past and the future.

Gila, on the other hand, was quite specific. She wrote — remember? — tell me all about yourself. What was. What is. What will be. She wanted to know everything. Her questions put me, as Mazal would no doubt say, in a cucumber. Which made me ponder: should I tell the truth, or be like one of my characters and create a fictional past for myself? I did both. Gila was interested in a three-dimensional schemata of a guy she was getting to know. And despite my inventions I told her more about my past than I had told anyone else. And next time I would spice it up even more. As I said before, in inverso fashion, fiction is the greatest truth.

And doing this would not bother me. Especially since Gila was a shut wooden door, silent as a golem, closed about her past.

I had no problem consorting with both of them. Patriarch Abraham had two wives; and later, after Sarah's death, he took a third. Poor Isaac had only one. That's what you get when you suffer a life-long stun from that near sacrifice and you can't do your own wife picking but your papa sends a trusted servant far away to choose your bride. And Isaac's son, Jacob, had four wives. King David — Umberto dei Rossi, at Roni's Friday night dinner, had called him a giant killer who loved God and women — had six mistresses, including wives and concubines, and even one married woman, Bathsheva, whose husband, Uriah, David sent out to the front lines to be killed. Their son, Solomon, following in his lusty dad's footsteps, and like a true oriental potentate, had scores and scores of wives, some say one thousand. One thousand is a bit much for me, perhaps 998 too much. I didn't mind rotating Mazal and Gila, but I certainly didn't want to be seen by one, as you know by now, while I was with the other. Gila seeing me with Mazal or Ma seeing me with Mu was a scenario I wanted to avoid.

Each young woman pleased me in her own way. I have used the word "austere" regarding Gila. Indeed, there was something austere about her, especially her face. That austerity rippled through her. It was apparent even in her walk, which for lack of a better word, had the slightest hint of a moving slim tree trunk. In fact, if you looked carefully, as I did, her walk didn't have a limp; she didn't drag one foot, but she ever so slightly favored her right foot, as if there was a clamp of timber on her left.

No heads swerved when Gila walked. Yet when Mazal walked, she couldn't help it, it just unconsciously flowed out of her, all the synonyms for femaleness, womanliness, desirability, Eros, sexiness, came like nectar from a flower. For her heads swerved, twisted, turned, forty-five degrees, ninety degrees, and even once, so fixated was this guy on her, three-hundred-sixty degrees.

Both of them had a magic. Mazal's was her belief in it; also in the erotic aura that came naturally to her. She was born with it and the damp forest floor sex smell that wafted, yes, there's that word again, wafted out of her. I hoped she never walked alone in the woods, for if she did an entire menagerie would sniff her out and follow her, from ant to anthropoid, from dove to dinosaur. And mushrooms too. Gila's magic was in her touch, witness the three Hebrew letters of *Shabbat* embedded in me. Wait! I'm forgetting. Mazal's touch had magic too. So maybe it was me. No matter who touched me, I interpreted it as magic.

Mazal seemed ready for procreation, child bearing and suckling infants. All you had to do was look at her and she'd be in the family way. Mazal would have children, one after the other; one each year. And if the timing was right, and adjustments were made for daylight savings time and leap year, even two in one year. Mazal was a kind of mama earth, ready and ripe for seeding and bursting with fruition.

For Gila I couldn't say the same. I once heard a pretty girl who radiated chill called the Ice Princess. That's too outré for Gila, but I think austere is right on the mark. She had an elegant, aristocratic aura. Gila's profile reminded me of Queen Nefertiti, with her sloe-eyed beauty that spoke of distance. I seem to be edging slowly, carefully and reluctantly to "sexless". But that's not quite so, because if Gila were sexless why would I be interested in her?

One always needs comparisons. Comparisons are like a cane for an old man or a crutch for a cripple. Needed. Gila was less sexy than Mazal, true. But she did have something. Beauty. A magical, handsome allure, an aura austere that drew you near.

Or had her *Shabbat* imprinted on my palm totally befuddled me?

Perhaps because of her impediment, let's not forget her locked tongue, Gila created, almost naturally, a distancing aspect to her personality, a shell, one of self-interest and necessity. And that insulated, encapsulated, whatever natural sexual charm she may have had.

Let's sum it up: if you stood Mazal and Gila, Ma and Mu, side by side, your eye would be pleased by them both, but your libido would bend, stretch, contort towards....

With Gila I had little to discuss; perhaps with the pad it would be easier. With Mazal I could argue about levels of belief, superstition. Even if the language interchange was a bit erratic it was lots of fun. About Gila's intellect I knew little. Yet it wasn't as if her mind drew me. There was a different current about her. It didn't have buzz; it didn't hum; it didn't sting. But it was there, magnetic in a way, but not erotic. She stirred a transparent affection, akin to embracing air, but yet that airiness had substance. I could put my hands around, I could embrace that enchanting (in) substantiality.

With Mazal I felt I was in the here and now. With Gila I felt I had entered a make-believe world, a faraway place and a reverse time zone. When she spoke to me by writing, I felt we were in a secret place, a land of silence where a finger could talk as it etched Hebrew letters on one's skin.

I was caught between two choices; the girls, that is. This one or that one. Me and Ma. Or Mu and Me. Felt there were two huge walls of water hovering, looming, on either side of me, like at the splitting of the Red Sea. If I would choose the one on the right, let's say her name was Gila, would the Mazal wall come crashing down on me? Or vice versa?

I don't know why I thought of that water wall analogy, but in retrospect my instinct was better than my thoughts. I concluded that either/or was ridiculous. There was another choice. Doing as did the Children of Israel — to go straight ahead, turning neither to the left nor to the right.

That too was an option, a fancier word than choice. If you can't have both walls, maybe you'll have none. But at least you won't get drenched.

But I should mention my dream. I dreamt I was ballet dancing with Mazal. Although she was what she was in real life, now she was light as a feather. I lifted her up, turned her upside down over my shoulder; she did a split with her legs up in the air. I got a whiff of her source. The Hebrew has a marvelous word for it, *makor*, that source which is the source of life and source of all desire. Sweets to the sweet and sweetiepies emerge. But in the middle of the dance, in dreamsudden scene shift, Mazal became Gila and she had no weight at all. And, more remarkable, she spoke, and what she said I understood, and she spoke so wisely I made a note to remember the wisdom of her words. But when I woke, I couldn't recall a word she said.

I wish I had some of Puck's magic dust to sprinkle on Gila to make her talk, but I knew that such wishes defy reality. We don't, alas, live in a world of make believe. Effect tags cause and two follows one and no one is born old and dies young.

12   Saying Goodbye

When we returned to my apartment from the train station Mazal told me, and she lowered her head as she uttered these words, as if ashamed of saying them:

"For last night in Venice moi dormir in other house, house where moi were till their daughter surprise come home and you moi inviter here."

"But why?" I shouted. At least I think I shouted; if I didn't shout I certainly raised my voice. "Now that's a surprise. A terrible surprise. I thought no room for you there. Daughter came home, suddenly."

"Moi sleep up standing in kitchen." Then she laughed, a deep, throaty laugh. "No no. Moi make laughy. Moi sleep one night above floor."

"But why? Tell me why."

"Because moi must to get use to non dormir with you."

She said this shyly and with such depth of feeling I threw my arms around her and kissed her. Still, I could have argued with her about not spending the last night with me but I did not. Perhaps had I been more assertive I could have persuaded her to stay. But I desisted because Mazal said it so fetchingly and gave such a touching reason.

"But I will take you to the airport."

"Oui. Certainment. Merci. But moi have request for light fever."

I put my hand on her forehead. "Fever? You want a bit of flu?

Maybe laryngitis?"

"Non. Other fever. You do me good thing. Like make me a fever, *s'il vous plait*."

"Ah. Favor. Okay. What kind favor?"

"For raisons sentiment before moi to airport, you meet moi by bench where we meet, bon? And then we to airport."

I have always distanced myself from acts of sentimentality. As from acts of superstition. But what was I to do? I think it would have hurt her had I said no.

"Okay. We meet there tomorrow. What time is your flight?"

"Two pm in after the noon. But moi must to be in airport at twelve."

"Fine. Then we meet at the bench tomorrow at eleven and I take you straight to airport."

Still—I felt it hovering between my heart and my brain— something, someone, somewhat told me: Don't go, don't go, don't go.

During the night that I was alone — and I felt that aloneness; it took me a long while to fall asleep — I thought about Mazal. I reprised the two or three clever answers that Mazal shot back at me during our contretemps at Roni's house, replies that surprised the wits out of me. The more I thought about Mazal the more I began to see her as a whole human being and not just as a sexy girl with enchantingly flawed English and an off-the-wall ideé fixe to prostrate herself on the grave of a long dead rabbi and pray for help. Mazal, I had to admit, had guts. She sought no one else's aid in solving her problem. She wanted to do it on her own. She had the independence of spirit to go by herself from Paris to a city where she knew no one and where she had never been before and with a limited budget too. And she would have gone by herself to the Padua cemetery had not a volunteer come along. And though Mazal's education was apparently minimal — she probably had not gone to college, perhaps only to one of those two-year post-high-school teachers seminaries, yet she felt the need and desire to see art at the Biennale.

We met on time. Mazal placed her two little bags on the far side of the bench and we sat down looking at each other. For a moment we were silent. Mazal's face, usually radiant with a kind of inner joy, even when she was talking about her problems back home, her face was now triste. That sadness reminded me of the dolor I had first seen on Gila's face. Mazal was pale and her dimples, no trace of them. I didn't know what to say; I guess neither did she. Then, spontaneously, we both stood. I put my arms around her and hugged her. Just then I felt a presence hovering near me, brushing me. It seemed like an angel's wing, but it was not beneficent, not a lacy, butterfly-wing caress; rather, it was an angry and rough graze and the surprise presence departed in a huff.

"Come, we're going to go to the airport in a way you never dreamed of."

Instead of going by bus we took a speedboat at St. Mark's Square, getting a last look at Venice.

On the boat, which occasionally rocked because of the waves, she said:

"Moi no golem."

I laughed. "Why you say that?"

"Recall? Youi invite moi to you house but no give address. Because if moi golem moi know you address. Because golem like you know everything."

Then she smiled, took my left hand, and pressed the palm

with the inscribed letters of *Shabbat* שׁבּת and pressed it to her face. It pleased me that she remembered my little joke; I had forgotten all about it.

At the airport we parted with a kiss, lips touching; but it was not a kiss, and even if it seemed like a kiss it was nothing like the kiss she had given me other night in my bed.

That kiss in the airport left me unfulfilled, grasping a handful of air. As if someone had shut the radio during the final minute of a Haydn symphony or blanked the screen just before the end of a film.

An emptiness swirled in me. I remembered the fire of Mazal's kiss as she rolled on top of me in my bed, the passion, yes, the fire in us at the Padua cemetery, and now I felt a minus fire, a cold blaze in my chest, my limbs, my head. And the chill of the airconditioned huge hall didn't help either.

Mazal did not ask me if I loved her and I did not ask her if she loved me.

A sinking feeling eddied in me when I cast a last look at her waving goodbye as she entered the terminal. Oh my God, I thought I didn't want to be drawn to her and I was drawn to her. I wanted to be drawn to that other her, to Gila, to Mu, whose left eye was lavender blue and right chartreuse green, who insinuated herself into me with three Hebrew letters on my palm and with pulses that came unannounced, pulsing pulses that spelled, Me Me Me.

And whose ghost had probably brushed me by the bench in protest with gruff, hair shirt wings.

13   Waiting by the Lido

Since it wasn't raining I waited for Gila outside the Lido Grand
Hotel on Lido island, the only part of Venice that had automobiles.
I waited outside in the sunshine, reprising for myself the famous
novella by Thomas Mann, most of which takes place inside the
hotel and out by the beach. I waited fifteen, twenty minutes, then
began a short walk, always keeping my eye on the front of the
hotel.

As I walked on the sand I thought of myself as Mann, writing
Death in Venice, having his hero, Tadzio, stay at the Lido Grand
Hotel, and me viewing the beach and the water through his eyes.

The minutes stretched into an hour. My heart pounded, irreg-
ularly. Disappointment set the rhythm off.

I waited.....and....

waited.....and.......

waited...

until....

Curt Leviant

I could wait...

no more, and so....

I returned to the mainland.

Maybe....

she misunderstood our rendezvous spot.

Maybe she thought we were to meet by a gondola station again.

I couldn't look for her for I did not know where she lived. I went from one gondola station to another, hoping to find her. Why I did that I don't know. We hadn't made plans to take a gondola again. It was a desperate attempt to turn back the clock.

And then it dawned on my why Gila had not shown up.

It was because of me. She had run off.

Away. Hurt. Distressed. And that's why she brushed her wrathful angel's wings over my skin.

14   Questioning Mo. His Surprising Reply

Remembering that both Gila and Mo were newcomers to Venice, and that Gila had traveled in Spain, was likely born there, and understood Spanish and Hebrew, and that Mo had been to Girona, Spain, had a slight Spanish accent and knew Hebrew too, and recalling my wild idea that if they didn't know each other, I would introduce them—I went to Mo's apartment.

"Aha," Mo said, opening the door after I had knocked. But he did not say, Nice to see you again.

He ticked his head up in typical Middle Eastern fashion, as if to say: What can I do for you? Or: What's on your mind? Or, with less civility: What's up?

After a polite greeting, I said, "I'd like to consult you. I have a question."

"Please ask."

"I appreciate your courtesy. Here's the story. There's a woman I've seen in the synagogue and in the *Shabbat* Kiddush courtyard who seems to be by herself. She doesn't talk to anyone and no one talks to her."

I was about to say that I had heard from someone that she had traveled to Spain. But if I said that it showed that someone had spoken to her. And if I said she wrote it down for me he would, if he were sharp, and I'm sure he is, he would say that means you saw her twice, for she would not write on *Shabbat*. So, to avoid getting all tangled up, I thought I'd say that since both were newcomers here perhaps he knew her. A flimsy connection, but still better than nothing.

Then I hesitated again. I wasn't keen to hear a snippety answer. Something like: Yes, sure. Just because two people in the Ghetto are new here they have to know each other.

And then a sensation that preceded my thoughts ran down my left shoulder to my arm, and from my arm to my left palm, which I clamped shut in his presence. I recalled the first time I met Mo we both used the same three words in reference to the old synagogue in Venice: history, continuity and sanctity. Mo had said that when he occasionally goes to the synagogue by himself he feels those three words on the palms of his hands. Just like I feel Gila's three letters for *Shabbat* on my palm. And this makes me feel a vague link to Mo, more on my skin than in my thoughts. And then before me I also see those three words that Gila had not written on me: "Words bind us."

In the midst of my thoughts I hear Mo say: "I still don't hear a question."

I didn't like his tone. Nevertheless, I asked him, still trepidatiously, fearing his expected sardonic retort, "Since both of you are newcomers here, do you... by any chance... know this mysterious woman?"

Mo's quick answer surprised me. In fact, there was a pleasant look on his face. That surprised me too. "But of course," he said. "What a question! Two people in this tiny Ghetto who are newcomers? How can they not know one another? Especially if they come from Spain. Of course I know her. That's my woman."

Oh, my God! His woman. And I had this wild, vague idea of introducing them. Good I hadn't told him I was socializing with his woman who may very well have been his wife. For once buttoned lips came to my aid. So that's where Gila was heading when she didn't want me to know where she was running to. No wonder she was so secretive about where she lived. And now, besides fearing that Mazal might see me with Gila, now I had to worry about another pair of spying eyes.

And more: again a set of three crucial words: That's my woman.

Was it possible she lived with him?

But, on the other hand, if she did, how come I didn't see her when I visited him the first time; and where was she now?

This probably means they lived apart. And if so, why? Why did this strange couple, if couple they were, live apart? Was it a kind of reverse osmosis? *Because* Mo was attracted to her, that's why he distanced himself.

I recalled *Decameron* and medieval folktales, Jewish and not, some of which featured concupiscent husbands, and others, lusty young wives married to pious old men. I thought of Mo and Gila as part of this narrative. She was the lusty wife who had run off with a younger fellow and then regretted her adventure. She asked her husband for forgiveness. He consented, said he would not abandon her but, for a while, they would have to live apart. And, meanwhile, as part of her penance, she was not to talk. Or maybe it was worsa vice — she was the one who had set that condition as punishment for her husband's womanizing. Until she gave the word, she wouldn't let him live with her under one roof and she wouldn't talk to him or to anyone else. Sexy medieval folktales were lots of fun. And variations on them that one imagined even more so.

Or maybe *because* they weren't married Mo observed a strict code of religious restraint no longer seen nowadays. An attitude like this was perfectly understandable, even thoroughly reasonable and admirable; that is, if you stood on your head and turned yourself inside out.

"Your woman?" I finally exclaimed. Now I wasn't shy. Now I said straight out, "You mean your wife."

Mo's face, despite the tiny blotches, remained crisp, unmoved. There was that haughty demeanor again. I knew that scornful look had to return sooner or later.

"She's not my wife," he said flatly. "Were she my wife I would have said, *My wife*, and not, *My woman*. I am precise in my language."

Now that's more like Mo. There's that combative tone again. Maybe not so much tone as choice of words and their placement in the sentence. And it's good he spoke English to me and not Hebrew, which doesn't distinguish between "my wife" and "my woman" but uses the same word: *ishti*.

Mo looked at me with a kind of ironic gleam in his eye as if he had bested me in a debate.

"Still, isn't it strange that no one speaks to her?" I said.

"Because they know her."

Because they know they don't speak to her. Here's a mystery that has to be unraveled.

Wait. Those last words of his echoed in my mind. I had heard them before. And my reaction had been the same. Yes. When I first met Roni and spoke to him at the *Shabbat* Kiddush and asked him about that woman and wondered why no one spoke to her. In his reply, the rabbi used the same words: Because they know her. What a strange place the Ghetto. Words float in the air. They start with one person and are echoed by another.

"What does that mean?" I asked him, on edge, fearing he might not answer.

"They know she won't answer so they don't talk to her."

I continued to play dumb. Made believe I was unaware of her essential flaw.

"Is she angry at them for some reason? Has someone insulted her? Hurt her feelings?"

"No."

"Then why won't she answer."

"Because she can't talk."

"Why is that? Is she mute?"

Mo didn't answer directly. With his hands folded on his chest and a slight change of tone, he asked:

"Do you not find her muteness strange?"

"In what manner?" I think I knew what he was referring to. And I also sensed he was slyly testing me. I had had the same question but I wanted him to articulate it. But had I asked it I might have gotten an unwelcome response.

"Well, isn't it highly unusual for someone who can't speak to hear perfectly well?" Mo said.

"That struck me too as strange....But it looks like you're leading into an explanation, Mo. So, please, I'd like to hear it." Then I added, "So she is mute."

"Technically. But it's not so much mute," he said in a perfectly amicable manner, "which is physical, but she cannot even make the slightest of sounds which other mute people can make, hence it is organic, systemic."

It was difficult to make sense of these simple but dense words. What was the difference between the two? I wondered. But at least he was answering politely.

"But still the question remains. Why can't she talk?" I finally said.

"Because ..." Mo said, repressing the "glad you asked" tone

in his voice, which was, however, subsumed into his multi-tonal, three-note, "Be-cau-ause..." He stopped for a moment to let me digest the three notes, then continued:

"... I made her," he said, adding to the thick layer of words spinning about me.

I was sure he wasn't using the American slang expression for sexual conquest. But then that presented another problem. Did he really mean what he was saying? I made her. Or perhaps he meant: I made her mute. That is, he was responsible for her defect. But if that were the case he wouldn't boast about it.

So there it was: another headline three-word enigma. I made her.

"You what?"

But Mo just looked at me. I had a hunch he wouldn't answer. He was purposely dragging out this seismic scenario. But I saw through him. Deep down, he was smiling, laughing, at me. Waiting for me to continue. Then, as more folktales raced through me, I realized:

"You m...m...mean, y...you..." I stammered.

"Yes."

These two exchanges, three of my words, one of his, filled many blank pages. Additional small talk, even big talk, wasn't necessary. In fact, it was superfluous. In fact, I think we could have said them silently, with raised eyebrows and eyes wide (me) and the slightest of nods (him).

"Wait a minute! A gol.... Are you the Maharal of Prague? Creating a g...?"

"No, I am not the Maharal," swiftly said. "How can I even compare myself to the great sixteenth-century Rabbi Loew, I who do not even come up to the edges of his tallit? But, yes, she is my creation. And as a golem she follows, she must follow, one cannot do battle with legend or undo history, there are no exceptions, she must obey and follow the rules that all golems follow. She can do everything but speak, for golems cannot talk. You know that, don't you? Or don't you?"

"I do. The Maharal's golem couldn't speak either."

"He followed the rules," Mo added. "And to be grammatically precise, in Hebrew the term for Gila is *golemet.*"

Was he being serious or parodic? Sometimes what he said could be interpreted in two ways, a kind of harnessed sarcasm that could also be seen as a good-humored comment.

"For she is not created by God but merely fashioned by a man of flesh and blood. Only the humans created by God have the gift of speech."

"Yes, I know that," I said. "We also know the Maharal of Prague fashioned the golem to help him with his domestic chores."

Now I began to tread carefully. Barefoot on broken glass.

"Can you tell me... Mo ... I mean, would it be an imposition..." I was groping my way, not wishing to offend him, that bright and lonely, that shy and facially marked man — hence, his occasional hauteur, which I understood — who himself deprecated his own self worth as a man of flesh and blood, "can you tell me why you made a golem? And especially a woman golem, which no one has ever made before?"

"And out of wood," Mo added proudly, "and not out of clay."

"Did you purposely make her with two differently colored eyes? What a brilliant touch!"

"No, sorry, that's not my doing. It just came out that way. Beautifully. Happily so."

"And you probably made her all alone and not with the help

of a committee like the Maharal's golem."

To this Mo did not reply.

"And very likely you didn't create her to become a serving girl and do housework."

"Well, that's what the legend holds. One must always follow legends," he said.

"And is the legend true?" I asked. "Sometimes legends hold a kernel of truth."

Again Mo was silent.

"Okay. Then perhaps you'll comment on this. You said you made the golem out of wood. Then how did the change to a human being come about?"

I spoke as though the dialogue had already been written and I was just reciting from the script.

"Little by little," he said, "like Pinocchio, she became a woman. The only thing that remained of her first state is her rather wooden walk."

"Yes. I noticed that..." And then I plunged sans discretion into the next question. "And you never thought of making her your wife?"

To my astonishment Mo answered right away and uttered the most personal, revealing words I had heard him say:

"Making her was enough. I am too ugly for a woman to love me."

I shook my head, disagreeing. His confession touched me and I wanted to say something to counteract those self-negating words.

"A man is what he perceives himself to be....You are wrong about your appearance, which is actually very noble and princely."

"And she's more like a sister."

"Yes," I said. Now it was my turn for unbuttoned sarcasm.

"Like the Song of Songs has it: 'My sister, my bride'." Just like the relationship I had earlier thought of with Gila.

But Mo did not react to this. Instead, he asked me, "Do you know the kabbalistic concept, the mystical concept of the Chariot."

"I know nothing of mysticism," I told him. "Even less than that."

"Good." And Mo gave a pleasant little laugh. "Then I can say what I want without being challenged. But what you just said itself has a patina of Kabbala, treading into the notion of less than nothing."

I shrugged.

"When one rides the mystical Chariot," Mo said slowly, "one can traverse time zones with ease."

"And languages?"

"Languages adhere to us like sunshine tans the skin. And, anyway, we Jews are good at languages."

But none of this satisfied me. So I did not desist from my earlier question. "So can you tell me why you made her?" I thought of politely adding, If you don't mind, but I deleted it.

Soon as I said this, and long afterwards, I realized I should not have asked this question. It wasn't discreet. It wasn't delicate. I was still having buttoning trouble. If you don't button your lip you become hostage to your tongue and you end up with your foot in your mouth. There. That's a lot of body parts — count 'em, four — involved in the simple act of trying to keep mum, three parts clustered at the top, just below the nose, and one at the bottom, ensconced in a shoe.

Who knows what secrets thoughts pulse and vibrate in a man if and when he has the ability to create a golem? And, anyway, am I, a thoroughly rational human being, am I to believe such an absurd assertion in the 21st century?

From such a small and wise and articulate man like Mo I was expecting a long and compelling answer. But Mo's answer was swift and to the point.

"No."

I heard that No and ran out. I ran out not because of that No, although that was the impression I must have given him. I ran out because now knowing who, what, Gila was, I knew what to do and I had to do it quickly. If Gila's gone, she's despondent. If she's despondent, she's desperate. If she's desperate, she's... About that I didn't even want to think, but I had a hunch where to find her.

I knew I had to run, but like in a bad dream the verb *running* subverted, sabotaged its own meaning. Everything turned to slow motion. In a nightmare you try to run, to move quickly, but you are unable to, and you feel you are slogging through thick mud, and you keep encountering people who hold you up, delay you, get in your way, but out of politeness you can't slip away from them.

Abramo Orsolini was one such man.

And I was another.

But first I ran to Roni, for I knew he had the key to the synagogue. He gave it to me, quickly, didn't ask why I wanted it, but told me two keys are needed. The second was at the Ghetto community office. Only when I was at the door did Roni throw an offhand question at me.

"By the way, do you know where Mazal is? Did she make it to the Padua cemetery?"

"I don't know," I said quickly. "Didn't she say at your Friday night dinner that she'll go back to France after visiting the cemetery?"

"I don't recall that," Roni said.

I made a neutral moue, thanked him for the key, and ran to the community offices.

On my way I met Abramo Orsolini, one of the community officials.

15   Getting the Keys

I thought I'd see Orsolini at his office right next to the synagogue. I knew who to ask for at the community office, for while still in the US I had had a few email exchanges with him pertaining to my apartment and I had met him once just soon after I arrived.

But there he was, walking on the street, holding a little folder.

"Shalom, Signor Orsolini," I said cheerfully.

"Ah, aren't you the writing Fellow?"

"Yes."

"Writing about our own Modena."

"Good memory, signore. Was supposed to do a full work, but I'm including him in a different way."

"Hmm."

"It's okay, it's okay," I said, seeing that he looked displeased. "Signor Ottolenghi wrote to me in his very first letter that a Writing Fellow has the freedom to change his topic. But that's another matter... What concerns me now, if you don't mind, I have to go to the synagogue and I need the other key." I waved the first one that Roni had given me. "The rabbi gave me this one. Can you help me?"

Orsolini patted his pockets. "I don't have it with me. Why don't you go up to the office and tell Angelina that you just met me and spoke to me. But what's the rush? You want to pray an early Mincha by yourself?"

I narrowed my brows, trying to assess if that last question housed a sarcastic jab. Of course, I didn't want to go into the entire story. I merely said:

"I want to check some Sephardic prayer books for certain passages."

And then I asked him a question there was no need to ask. I had been worried that Orsolini might delay me with banalities and here I was, in a rush, putting impediments in my own way. But I was so excited by what Mo had told me I had to share it with someone. So why didn't I tell this to Roni? Good question. I was afraid he would laugh. Think me naive. And, anyway, I had to move quickly.

"Do you know Mo?" I asked Orsolini.

"Who's Mo?"

"The man who lives near the synagogue who came here recently. You know, he has a beard and wears a little cap."

"Oh, him. Yes, sure, we know him."

"So aren't you impressed that one of your community members…" I wanted to stop but I couldn't. I shouldn't even have said the words I had already uttered. Maybe Mo doesn't want it known. But I couldn't button my lip… "created a golem?"

"First of all, he's not a member of our community."

But Orsolini did not continue with a second of all. Evidently, he knew all about the golem. My remark prompted no surprise. He just looked at me with dancing eyes; no need to record their color, which wasn't as memorable as Gila's two-colored set, one chartreuse, the other lavender.

Anyway, I had to get moving, go to Gila. Why am I standing here, staring at Orsolini? For a moment he reminded me of Mo. With his head tilted to a side and lips compressed, Abramo's face showed he felt sorry for the poor simp—me, or better, Me, the hero of the truevelistic work being composed in, about, Venice—

who was taken in by all this nonsense. Had he known Yiddish he could have asked me: So you believe this *bobbe-mayse*? This fairy tale. This legend? This literary hoax?

And to accent his point his finger made circular motions by his ear, the almost universal sign for looniness.

"Did he come to Venice with her?" I wanted to know. Why was I stretching out this conversation. I was anxious to get to my destination before it — I was too late.

This Orsolini considered a serious question, for he replied:

"We didn't notice. Maybe he picked her up in Padua. They don't always go together. Also he doesn't come to shul."

"That I know. Mo told me this when I first met him...." I watched him closely to see his reaction to my next remark. "I think you know why he stays away."

But Orsolini's expression did not change.

"That's the way he is," he said dryly. Then he added, "Persnickety."

Now that word surprised me; yes, in fact impressed me.

"Where'd you get that Americanism?"

"I looked it up," he said with just a hint of a smile in his eyes.

"But he's not persnickety. There's a reason for his not being sociable and not coming to shul. He's sensitive about his face. The tiny blotches. The disfigurement. Didn't you realize that?"

Orsolini was not moved. I tried to change the subject.

"By the way, do you know how he supports himself? Does he have a profession?"

"Didn't you ask him?" Orsolini countered.

"Our conversation didn't head in that direction."

"Well, he calls himself a Hebrew poet," said Orsolini.

Curt Leviant

"Mo, a poet?" I mused out loud and a feeling of unease came over me.

I looked at the man in front of me and continued:

"Do you by any chance which city in Spain Mo lived in?"

I barely got the words out, for there was a strange pressure in my chest which took my breath away. I just managed to utter "in". Nevertheless, I did realize I had omitted the word "know". But Orsolini understood the intent of my question, which proved that we can communicate with far fewer words than we think.

"He said he came from Malaga... And why do you insist on calling him Mo?"

"It's not my call," I said. "That's how he introduced himself to me."

"It's probably a nickname he uses," Orsolini said.

"So what's his name?"

"It's Shlomo."

Again that fist closing in on my breathing, that tightening in my chest.

Oh, my God! Shlomo...

"You said Shlomo?"

And I heard Orsolini say, "I said Shlomo."

"I thought Mo was short for Moshe, Moses."

"Well, it's not. His name is Shlomo."

"And he's from Malaga."

"Malaga." Dryly said, without music, without emotion.

Oh, my God! Shlomo and Malaga. Now shivers ran down my spine and a thick pulsing in my head, not hurtful; then an explosion of light, glowing electrons shaped like Hebrew letters. The letters settled. Jig and saw were no longer separated. Now the jigsaw pieces came together. Had I known earlier — Shlomo, poet, Malaga — I would have at once made the connection with Gila. With Mu.

I knew well the story of the eleventh century Spanish Hebrew poet, Shlomo ibn Gvirol, from Malaga, who died, like all geniuses, like Mozart, Schubert, Mendelssohn, Gershwin, in their thirties, and who, in his own words, in one of his lachrymose Hebrew poems, called himself "small, sickly, ugly". Like I told Gila, I knew only a few poems of Shlomo's. The legend of his short, poor life fascinated me more than his poetry. Legends, stories, near make-believe, that for me was the truest poetry.

And this Shlomo surely never married and, very likely, to have a companion, created the female golem, the first female golem in the history of golemhood or golemdom, even if only of wood, and even if only to watch her clean the rooms. But my instinct tells me she didn't have to do much cleaning. Little by little the wood evanesced and turned to flesh. To lovely, mute, Gila.

And Shlomo ibn Gvirol himself became a legendary figure, famous for centuries in Spain and elsewhere in the Jewish world. Even modern Spain, under Franco, was proud of this famous Sephardic poet and philosopher with deep roots in Spain, for the regime commissioned an impressive larger-than-life statue of ibn Gvirol that stands in one of Malaga's grand public squares.

In fact, before deciding on the Leona da Modena project, I had briefly considered ibn Gvirol and his female golem. It was a unique and fascinating story, but I didn't know how to connect them to Venice, one of the required anchors for any literary project undertaken by a Venice Fellow. It never occurred to me to bring them to Venice and set a story there.

What was going on here?

Curt Leviant

My whole life in Venice was tilting, slipping. It was as if the smooth ride I was having on a gondola suddenly....But wait. That's just what had happened to me when I was with Gila. I wanted to use a gondola ride as a metaphor — and I had become the metaphor. And now my time zone was askew. I was foundering in a new medium, neither land nor water, but in a soft-edged melting time span that hovered between past and present, here and there.

Then I shifted the conversation.

"She seems older."

"That's his choice." Orsolini tilted his head. "Sometimes older women like younger guys and younger men go for older women."

"We have to remember she can't speak," I said.

"Some husbands would say that's a superb attribute."

I disregarded Orsolini's attempt at humor.

"I think it's very important to remember that she can't speak," I said. "That's a crucial fact here if she's a golem."

"Her not speaking still doesn't make her a golem. It could all be a show. A few of us here think that if someone came up behind her and gave her a good pinch in the rear, you'd soon see and hear her speak and squeal quick enough. And in Italian too. Golem, indeed! I mean, you're a rational man, for goodness sake, aren't you?"

"So you think it's all sham?" I asked. Tell him she's legit, I hear a voice telling me. Show him the *Shabbat* on your palm, the audience is shouting. Still, I held back.

"Sham? What is this sham?"

"You know persnickety but not sham?"

"My dictionary stopped at 'p'." And here Orsolini smiled.

"Sham is make-believe. Fakery."

"Could be." Orsolini looked thoughtful for a moment. "Once you create a legend you have to abide all the rules of the legend."

Not bad, I thought. Nicely said. In fact, echoing Mo's words.

"Besides not being able to speak, does this woman seem normal to you?"

"I would say so," Orsolini said, "but usually normality is determined by hearing someone speak… How does she strike you?"

That he was asking me my opinion pleased me.

"Normal as far as I can tell. Her walk is a bit stiff though."

I ran to the community office and relayed to Angelina what Abramo Orsolini had told me.

"But first you have to get the key from the rabbi," she said.

I showed her the key in my hand.

"Oh. Then here is the second one. The rabbi's key is for the top lock and this one is for the one below it. Please bring it back to me when you are finished."

But instead of rushing to the synagogue next door, I...

Curt Leviant

16 A Nagging Question

...ran back to Mo. I shouldn't have come back. I should have been running to Gila, but now that I knew who Shlomo was I had to ask him another question. It wasn't even personal. It was more metaphysical; well, maybe a bit personal too.

I knocked three times, three short taps, and walked in without waiting for him to reply. Mo was reading what looked like a parchment manuscript. Soon as he saw me he rose.

"You are Shlomo. I just heard. Why didn't you tell me?"

"You didn't ask."

I wanted to judge Mo beneficently, even though he annoyed me at times. He probably didn't want to be brusque but he couldn't help it. It was built into his makeup, keyed into his genes. It stemmed from the tiny blotches on his face, the smoothed over excrescences on his cheeks that he tried to hide with his little beard.

"Still, you introduced yourself as Mo. Why?"

"Shyness. Modesty. Privacy." He pronounced the last word the British way, with a short "i". And there it was again. Another three-word cluster.

"But you weren't shy about Gila."

"So you know her name. Why didn't you tell me?"

"You didn't ask."

I didn't let Shlomo know how distressed I was by his earlier refusal to tell me why he had made the golem. But I didn't want our exchanges clouded with antagonism. So I asked him the question I had planned to ask, one that might intrigue the philosopher in him, in a mild, soft voice:

"Can you tell me, Shlomo, do you have any idea why you are here?"

He looked, no, not looked, he stared at me, hammered his glance into me, as if to tell me that I had breached etiquette with that question. There I go again. Maybe I *should* get a zipper for my lips. Although Shlomo was sharp-tongued, he wasn't the sort to blatantly burst out with — Mind your own business.

"You asked me that the first time you saw me."

"I did? I have no memory of that questions at all."

"Yes. So it seems you forgot my answer."

"Sorry. If I asked, I guess I forgot your answer. What was it?"

"I forget too. But it was something like, There are reasons for everything."

A cryptic response. I was hoping for a longer answer, even one with a mystical slant. Maybe he did that purposely, to add to the mystery about him. Which made me think that perhaps skeptics like Abramo Orsolini had a point. About Mo, and about Mu too. But then how do I account for that *Shabbat* on, in, my palm?

Torn was I, am I, and I am still, as you can see, fra realita and impossibilita. But. Still. Yet. Nevertheless. Maybe. Perhaps one can still combine the two in this world.

"Have you written any new poetry?"

"I'm working on something...But listen..." And here he began reciting.

I didn't understand all of it.

"This one is one of my famous ones," he said proudly.

But with the skeptic Orsolini hovering in back of my mind, I

Curt Leviant

thought even if he recites ibn Gvirol's poetry by heart it's no proof he is who he says he is. So maybe the skeptics are right after all.

And then I shifted on the chessboard and made a little knight-like leap, saying as politely as I could:

"Your previous answer, I couldn't fathom it. So I'll ask again why you came to this era, to this place."

"Not again. A third time," Shlomo said. "You like groups of three, don't you?"

"Like you. History, continuity, sanctity... Shyness, modesty, privacy... That's my woman... There's three of your own groups of three." And I smiled, just to show him I wasn't being contentious.

This time he didn't answer. But I like to think his answer might have been that it was done for me, for my sake, for my benefit. To add color, intrigue, substance to my Venice project. Here we go again. Two more clusters of threes. And the hint was in those three words that both of us uttered about the great Venice synagogue, the ones he recited the first time we met, why we both loved that shul. History, continuity, sanctity.

This bound us, seemed to me, tied us together.

And then a frisson of fright overtook me and I had the wild thought that if I'd ask Shlomo one more time why he came here he'd look me in the eye and say three words:

"Because I'm you."

Without another word,

I took off.

Without saying goodbye.

I ran quickly.

To the shul.

Hoping that I'm

not too late.

Because it was me. I was the cause of her fleeing. I had hurt here. And now I had to find her before ... I didn't even want to think about that possibility.

Curt Leviant

17   In the Attic

I raced. Didn't look left, didn't look right. Saw a familiar face. I think it was the office clerk, Angelina. Didn't stop. Till I got to the front door of the synagogue. Inserted the key. Went into pocket for other. Empty. Not there. In panic, searched all my pockets. Nothing. Looked again. Lost it. How could I have lost the second key? An absurd thought roiled my mind. Shlomo took it. Didn't want me to go to the synagogue. To meet up with Gila. But could he know my destination?

Considered banging on the door. Knew that was futile. In desperation twisted the handle and pushed.

The door opened.

It had been open all along.

If not, how could Gila, if indeed she is up there, have gotten in?

In the foyer stood a vase filled with roses, roses red and white. I took the roses and walked up the old steep narrow wooden stairs. Each step I took made each step i took steeper. Each step I took made more steps. Like in a bad dream I was hurrying so slowly, in the lugubrious pace of a turtle. Taking the three tight flights to the attic, to the former women's gallery, where I knew I'd find Gila.

And there she was, lying on the floor, on her back, in the narrow space between the last row of the three rows of joined seats and the small windows that faced down into the Ghetto.

Her eyes were closed. My first thought was, Oh God, I'm too late. Was she so upset at seeing me hugging Mazal that she wanted to end her life? That she had come up to the attic because she wanted to return to her original wooden state? Can love denied be equal to life denied?

But then I noticed she was breathing, evenly, slowly, the breaths far apart, like a machine whose power is running down. I placed the bouquet by her head.

Next to her hand lay her little writing tablet. Some words were still on it.

I began to read. It was written in the third person, as if what was happening was happening to someone else:

"She lay down, on her back, looking up at the ceiling which she did not see because she half closed her eyes. It began in her legs, because that's where she wanted it to begin. The life still ebbed in them, but then a feeling of heaviness, languor, thickness commenced in her toes, her ankles, her feet. The woodenness. She was returning. As Adam had returned. We start one way, she reflected, not with sadness, but with wisdom, and we become another, and then we must return the way we began. Her fingers and hands would be next, she knew. For a moment she lifted her hands, opened her eyes, and gazed at her fingernails. Then she replaced her hands at her sides. At that moment she heard footsteps."

Her face was pale; no color in her fingers; her fingers white a snow.

But at least she was alive.

"Gila! Gila!" I shouted.

18   In the Attic, Continued

She sat up. For a moment she looked at me, dazed, her face stiff. She was re-entering, from a distant planet, and her eyes were adjusting. Then her features softened; the color came back to her cheeks, and the two colors to her eyes, chartreuse and lavender.

"It's me, Gila," I said. "I'm so glad I found you in time." I should also have said the same line without the last two words, but I thought of that only later.

I gave her the bouquet and for a moment felt I was acting out a Chagall painting. She took it, sniffed deeply, and, not as a rejection of my gift, for there was a gentle smile on her face, threw the flowers into the air, as if she wanted the entire space of the air filled with rose petals. The petals floated up, then down, like red and white snowflakes. So many petals floated I could not see Gila's face, mottled with the colored flakes, the rose petals and the shadows of the petal flakes joining in the petal shower.

And with the petals slowly descending I imagined a ballet. Or perhaps I didn't imagine it. Perhaps I stood behind her like a danseur, lifting her up from a sitting position and holding her slim waist, lifting her with ease. We mimed a courtship as she floated up and came down slowly, her short dress billowing, she floating slowly like the rose and white rose petals still descending about us.

Then she sat down. But I, I was still standing.

The quiet up here where silence is the norm. The thin air of the attic. The woody, musty smell of the antique dust motes. The silent hum of the rounded seats where women had sat hundreds of years ago. The blue sky through the pale glass still transparent; for centuries the windows never opened.

Gila regarded me with half-closed eyes. She looked intently through her half-closed eyes that were perfectly relaxed, her brows not at all furrowed, and said —

Of course she didn't say it, but here is what she did: she took my left hand, spread open my fingers, and pressed her thumb on the *tav*, the last letter of the three-lettered *Shabbat*. Now the two other letters, *shin* and *bet* remained, that spelled *shev* — sit.

And so I did, on the old wooden floor next to her. Despite their age the floorboards were smooth as though set in place yesterday. Not a bump or dip in them. She pointed to her eyes, shut them, and then pointed to me. I shut my eyes.

She pressed down on all these letters. Again I felt a thrum, a mild vibrato in my hand that coursed through all my body, and I sensed her words:

"Why? Why? Why? Why didn't you let me sleep? I was prepared for that sweet wine sleep forever, you don't know how delicious is that temporary doze that lasts through eternity with warm snowflakes slowly drifting over me as I float slowly gliding into a sleep that gives no waking, have you ever entered a hot tub very tired after a day's work and closed your eyes relaxing in the bone- and nerve-numbing warmth and your eyes are shut in that captivating elixir before sleep and, embracing you, head back, you let yourself melt into the warm water that's the sleep I want and you...."

It sounded like she said, the sleep I want and you... meaning that she wants me too. But that "and" was really a "but". She wanted sleep but I came along and....

Curt Leviant

I opened my eyes. Her eyes a light of anger in them, but in her brow still not a furrow....Now she wrote in her pad: "and now you interrupted it, drove away the wine warmth, broke...how did you find me?"

I don't know how the words I said came to me: I didn't plan them. But as soon as she said "find me," from the depth of me I burst out with:

"The heart has better vision than the eyes."

And I meant it. There was no caginess, no false rhetoric in my words, even though the sentiment is sort of borrowed and the words recast to fit my manner of speaking.

Gila still hadn't released her thumb from the words she had imprinted on my palm. With her other hand she wrote:

"You mean that?"

Soon as Mo told me you were gone I knew exactly where you'd be, I was about to say, when/then I restrained myself. Perhaps if she knew what I knew about her she would feel discomfited. The balance between us would change. Vis-a-vis me she might feel diminuted, a creature originally of wood, a golem, and me, a full-fledged — at least in my estimation — human being. So I did not utter the words I was about to say. I was getting better, learning. Learning how to button my lip. And I was glad I was able to hold myself back from blurting out words I should not have said, not now, anyway.

"You mean that?"

Gila didn't say it again but I heard it again and I had to reply.

Now there was a (im)perceptible shift between us. She had spoken, in her way. Now I was the one mute of tongue. I gave her a short answer. I pointed to my heart, then, with my thumb, made an outgoing motion. Then I repeated those two gestures, pointing to my mouth, to say:

What enters and comes out of my heart is the same as what enters and comes out of my mouth. In speech it would be: what comes out of my mouth reflects my feelings.

Even shorter: my mouth and my heart are one. No forked tongue. I mean what I say.

And in answer to her question, shortest:

"Yes," I finally said.

Whether it was the gesture or the Yes, maybe one, maybe the other, maybe both, but at this a light suffused her face, pale no more, a roseate, life-aborning roseate glow returned to her skin, as if, indeed, the just-described warm bath instead of putting her to sleep injected some needed warmth to the snow flake drowse that had bound her soul.

Now her eyes were wide open. I couldn't take my eyes off her eyes. My eyes darted from one eye to the other. From the chartreuse, now brighter light green, to the lavender, now a brilliant lilac purple. In each burned a different light. A mute fire, intense in each eye.

"You heard of St. Exupery's book, *Little Prince*?" I asked her.

She shook her head.

"He said something similar there. 'One sees clearly only with the heart. What is essential is invisible to the eye'."

I sat alongside of her, facing her, my hip next to hers. Her legs stretched north; mine, south. I put my arms around her and hugged her. She twisted toward me and embraced my shoulders. She kissed me on the lips of her own accord and I heard a little sigh, an exhalation that was more than a breath. I could swear it had a bit of vibrato, something like the foreshadow of sound.

Curt Leviant

This has never happened before, were the words that flew through my mind. But I felt the feeling first and only afterwards did the feeling become a series of five words: this has never happened before.

Shlomo had tried to explain the difference between physical and systemic muteness. I was beginning to understand. If it's merely physical, a mute person can make some kind of sound, howbeit inarticulate. Was the vibrato I had just heard a sign of an impending change? ˙

I still don't know if Gila knew what I knew about her. If she knew what Mo had told me about her. Now I'll call Mo by his full name that reverberates throughout Jewish history: Shlomo ibn Gvirol, or Gabirol, that sad, lonely, ill and tragic genius who plucked words out of Moses's fiery bramble and put them into verse without getting burned. As he himself admitted, Mo was his disguise name so that people would not recognize him.

Now was the time, I thought. Now is the time to do what I had planned to do. To initiate and not just react. And so I brought my mouth to hers. She closed her eyes. I kissed her lips and then, parting them with my tongue, I sensed a tiny something under her tongue; it felt like stiff paper or parchment, like the one I had felt in her mouth in the cafe after the gondola ride. I withdrew it with my lips.

Gila fell limp in my arms, head back in a dead faint, her face waxen, hands pale, fingers gray white.

I looked at the tiny piece of parchment, no bigger than a pinkie nail, inscribed with minuscule Hebrew letters. I strained to see and finally made out the four letters of the holy name of God, the Tetragrammaton, the *yud*, the *hay*, the *vav*, the *hay*, the way it is handwritten in the Torah, the ineffable Name which only one man, the High Priest, would pronounce only one day of the year, on Yom Kippur, and only in one place, the Holy of Holies of the Holy Temple in Jerusalem.

"Oh, my God!" I cried out, knowing at once what it was and why it was there. At once, I returned it to her mouth, beneath her tongue.

Gila snapped back up, completely revived. The color returned to her cheeks, nose, fingers.

For a moment I had removed from Gila the life stuff that Mo had put into her when he created her. As soon as it was back in her mouth she was normal again. For Shlomo had learned very well and mastered the tradition of golem-making, using an older way of bringing a golem to life, very likely a more ancient kabbalistic method. The Maharal of Prague had walked seven times around the golem one way and seven times the other. In an old silent film version of the golem story, the Hebrew word for truth, אמת, made up of three letters, *alef,* א, *mem,* מ, *tav,* ת — is inscribed into the golem's forehead, bringing him to life. When the *alef,* standing for the first letter of God's name, is removed, only the letters *mem* מ and *tav* ת , which spell the word מת, *met,* dead, are left — and the golem expires.

Now I could get a closer look at her forehead to see if there was a tiny inscription there, made up of *aleph, mem, tav,* strangely, or not so strangely, perhaps mystically, yes, that's what it is, the first, the middle and the last letter of the Hebrew alphabet. Another three-letter word that Mo had indited there to vivify her just as Gila had revivified me with her three-letter word, shabbat, onto my skin, both of which ended with the last letter in the Hebrew alphabet, the *tav.*

Yes, I wanted a closer look at her forehead, but I wanted to kiss her too, on my own, and not just as my beloved Mama would say in Viennese, for the sake of "eigennutz," self-interest. But upon reflection I must confess that I kissed her to draw near her forehead, to see if the word אמת *emet, truth,* was indeed inscribed there. So I guess it was "eigennutz" after all. But in getting close I did not see any Hebrew word on Gila's forehead. Once more I kissed her soft, pink, well-formed, welcoming lips.

Just then something fascinating, and stirring, dawned on me. And again that frisson, a kind of spiritual chill rolled over me. In *golemet* the word *emet* was embedded. So Gila didn't have to have that word on her forehead, tiny script or not. It was contained in her essence; in Gila it was systemic, like the systemic muteness that Shlomo had described. And "cemetery" too had *emet* within it. In Jewish lore the World-to-Come, restricted real estate for the righteous dead, is called *olam ha-emet* — the True World. Coincidentally, "cemetery" also contains the Hebrew word *met*, "dead."

Now Gila showed me her pad and, with a wise, knowing look, slid it away from her on the floor. Purposely. As if to say, I no longer need this. She pointed to my ear and wagged her index finger slowly a couple of times, telling me to listen carefully.

Then she said; then she spoke.

I said, she spoke. You hear it right.

Mark it.

She spoke, saying; saying a flood rush of words:

"Shalom. There are lots of things I can say but I don't know if I have the words to say them. But I will only say three words: love undoes impediments. For love the words come by themselves, untutored, unrehearsed, in back of your mind or back of your throat. Love unbinds the tied, frees the frozen tongue. Under my tongue I tasted love. For love quickens. Love transports. Love loosens the bonds of travail. Love gives voice to man and song to birds. At love even fawns will speak. And am I not better than a doe?"

My mouth was open. She looked at, through me, into a beyond she was seeing with her gift of speech. That same distant look I had noticed the first time I saw her sitting opposite me in the women's section of the great Venice synagogue on a Sabbath morning, staring out and above, into a beyond far removed from the pages of the Siddur she held in her hand.

You are better than a doe, I didn't say, for who am I, a small writer of prose, to interrupt the poetry of this artist who is sharing her first song with me? Were I to sit with quill in hand, with pen or pencil, never in three and thirty years would I be able to compose such moving words on love.

"Love turns wood to flesh and makes the halt run free."

Her face was transcendent.

Have I said she sat up? If I did I forgot. Forgot because of the mesmerizing light of her eyes. One eye and the other. She sat up, shook herself, as if with that shake she shook off the longed-for sleep. She sat up. She got up. Rose from a sitting position, seemingly without using her hands. At least I didn't see her using her hands. Gila sprang up as if there was no intermediary resting point between sitting and standing. She sat up, she got up, she sprang up like a gazelle and took me by the hand. She took me by the hand and led me down the steep dark oak steps, the old narrow staircase that led down from the synagogue's no longer used women's gallery in the attic, walking slowly with me, not like a somnambulist but fully awake, being very cautious while descending those rather high dark wooden steps, but her words, *be careful,* were sent to me through her fingers into mine in no specific language, for words that throb like pulses do not know what language they are in, if Hebrew, English or Spanish.

"I knew," I told her outside, "that you'd have a musical voice, on the sultry side, rather low, like a clear oboe in the low register. As befits a handsome woman."

"But you disappointed me," she countered. "You hugged that pretty girl."

So it was Gila that day. I sensed it. Felt her rough, angry wings brushing me.

"It was just a friendly hug," I said lamely, feeling for the first time in my life what "lamely" meant. "She was returning to Paris."

So that's why you didn't show up for our Lido rendezvous, I didn't say, for I knew the answer.

And thinking of Ma gone, Mod flew into my mind, as if to say, I'm watching you. At which I said boldly, "You're gonna be surprised, Leone da Modena, at the role I'm gonna give you. Surprised and pleased, Mod, you'll be."

On our way from the synagogue, Gila didn't have to lead me. I didn't have to guide her.

We both knew where to go.

19   What Happened in Shlomo's Apartment

It seemed to me that Gila had sung that song of love to me, talking for the first time in her life, enjoying the miracle of her rebirth. She had defied reality, contravened folk tradition, come out of her golemhood, and begun to speak. As she said, love was the transformative key. No longer did she need God's name on a sliver of parchment under her tongue.

Gila and I walked from the synagogue to Shlomo's apartment. Gone was her slightly off-rhythm wooden amble.

On our way I looked up and see, in the sun-bright lavender sky, low flying, as if especially for me, that large grey backward moving bird with white fuzz above its tiny sad eyes, paddling casually, casually paddling its wings. Perhaps it was it who turned the time for my encounter with the past.

But Gila looked straight ahead. She had not seen the bird.

I wanted to ask her if she knew how she was made but I didn't dare. On the other hand, if I don't I'll regret it later and berate myself for not asking this crucial question. On the third hand, why should I remind her of a possibly unpleasant experience, and if not unpleasant, then surely uncomfortable?

I wanted to ask her if she missed childhood. But how can one miss something one didn't have? It would be like asking me, an only child, if I missed having a brother or a sister. How does one have a life that begins in mid-life, with no parents, no relatives, no friends, no memories? No wonder sadness was etched into her face.

I wanted to ask her how she felt when she was born, when she woke up. Did she have baby thoughts, or did she think at once like a grownup? And in a kind of waking dream, I imagine her not saying but writing her response: "It's like waking up after a deep, swift sleep, like after an injection of an anesthetic, that's me, waking up as an adult, fully grown, full of knowledge. If I tried, I could even come up with some childhood-like memories, but no one asks me and I don't talk about my past."

She had mentioned nothing of the gift she might give me. That elusive *there may come a time...* But I wasn't going to ask her now. Now that she was transformed. I realized it was likely a poem of Shlomo's. But now wasn't the time. That time may come later.

Now at Shlomo's door. I took a deep breath, heart pumping double time, wondering what Shlomo's reaction would be when he saw Gila — and me with her.

At the stone doorpost I looked at that indentation of a mezuza that I had noticed the first time I came to Mo's house right after I entered the Ghetto of Venice. But now Mo had been revealed to me in the full panoply of his fame. For him I had another round of questions. What did he do all day? Did he study? Write poetry? And in what language? Did he have friends? Can he move backwards in time? Or doesn't his mystical Chariot have a reverse gear? Shlomo still puzzled me. And from his vague answers it still wasn't clear why he had chosen Venice.

Gila didn't knock. She just opened the door and walked right in.

"Shalom," she said, loud and clear.

Shlomo, sitting at his desk, quill in hand, jumped up soon as he saw us. I watched him closely. His face looked strained, the blotches starker; his brows narrowed, as if trying to gauge the sound, the voice he had just heard, and to also wonder about our coming together. But, obviously, her speaking overrode other questions.

"Shalom," Gila said again.

The usual depiction for surprise, astonishment, is an open mouth, jaw dropping. But Shlomo's eyes just widened, his lips barely parted.

He said only, "How? Where?"

But Gila didn't answer; perhaps she didn't want to discuss the details.

Just then something happened.

To me.

Soon as I saw Shlomo and Gila together for the first time. A blow without the blow. An insult to the psyche. Insult in the medical sense, not impudence or discortesia. I was there with them but felt removed, like that iconic atom that scientists had discovered that could be in two places at the same time. I was in the room with Shlomo and Gila but also up in the synagogue attic looking down at them from the window. At that instant my closeness to Gila suddenly evaporated.

For a moment, as if I were a neutral observer, I thought in the third person, like the paragraph-long third person narrative by Gila I had just read in the attic:

He felt a short circuit go through him. It was Gila's doing, he knew. First she turned on the juice, now she shut it. Or maybe it wasn't that. It was this: seeing Gila and Shlomo, the two of them as one, cut the emotional tie in him. An old rubber band suddenly snapping. With Shlomo, he could hold her hand, embrace her, kiss her lips. But seeing Shlomo and Gila together now, the maker and

Curt Leviant

the maid, he felt disconnected. In the other half of his atom-in-two-places mode, he was in a semi-sleep, a drugged haze, hovering in that mist that blocked clear, sharp, unmitigated vision.

But was my vision any clearer now?

I saw Shlomo looking at me; then he turned to Gila and said, "Come."

I don't know if he meant both of us or just Gila, but I went too.

We followed him to another room.

In so doing I noticed two things. One: Mo did not take Gila's hand. And two: perhaps because of the astonishment of seeing Gila in her new state, Mo's usual testy responses and snippety attitude seemed to have melted away.

The room we were now in was bare of furniture except for a shoulder-high wooden armoire of a stunning darkly turquoise color. From it Shlomo removed something that looked like a few sticks attached to white cloth and held together with a bit of string. Then we returned to the first room.

Meanwhile, something inordinate had taken place. It fit in perfectly with the magic of Venice, reflections in water of old golden buildings, reflections you can touch but not hold.

What was formerly a little space wherein Mo had his writing table, the sort of room that slick American realtors would cleverly call cozy, this cozy little room had undergone a change. As if four assistants' hands had pushed all four walls back, and the tallest among them had also raised the roof.

This was the large, celebratory room where the three of us, Mo, Mu, and Me were now gathered.

Shlomo put those few sticks with the white cloth attached from the other room on his writing table and untied the string. I now saw four long hand-carved mahogany poles that supported an embroidered white canopy. By its sheen it looked like silk. This was obviously a portable *chupa*, a wedding canopy ready for use. But who and where the bride and groom? We possibly had a rabbi, for Shlomo ibn Gvirol too may have been a rabbi, like the other great Hebrew poets and thinkers from medieval Spain, like Yehuda Halevi and the Ibn Ezra that Mazal had mentioned at Roni's Friday night dinner in support of her superstitious contentions.

But wait. Seeing me, Shlomo probably concluded he better make what he considered his possession possessed. So he wanted to get the ceremony over and done with and quickly make Gila, now a full-fledged woman, his bride. And I was here as witness, for a witness was needed for a marriage ceremony, the same role I had assumed Shlomo would assume.

And while so thinking, I imagine that all those years they had been together this—in his own words, remember?—"small sickly, ugly man," had never expressed any love, not even affection for Gila, likely afraid of rejection; not even dreaming that by giving her life she would reciprocate gratitude by liking this talented poet and philosopher.

However, Shlomo's haste could also be interpreted in another fashion. Looking at Gila and at me, Mo was sensitive enough to realize what had happened between us and wanted to certify it in a typical Jewish manner: stand under the chupa with your chosen one.

But all this is speculation. I really knew nothing of what was happening. But then came a sudden thought: if a real rabbi would be needed, we have one ready and waiting: Rabbi Leone da Modena.

Shlomo stretched out one of the poles to Gila, one to me, and kept one for himself.

I don't know who was the first to start the circuitous parade, semi-walk, semi-dance, he, Gila, or me — but soon enough all three of us were chanting love verses from the Song of Songs and dancing around an invisible point. Despite the fact that four people were needed to hold up the portable chupa, it didn't droop; in fact, the white silk canopy above us was stretched above us nice and flat, with just the three of us holding the chupa's four mahogany poles.

But no one was in the center, no bride in the middle around whom the wedding revelers, groom and other close celebrants, are marching. Here, with the speed of dancers, the circle moved quickly; we gave the impression that all of us were in the middle; but who was who was hard to tell.

While walking under this canopy, I felt it was the same airy canopy that had draped itself over Gila and me the first time we took a walk. That same diaphanous cupola, that private bower of whipped fine gauze, but this time it was a bower we all could see. And as soon as we walked under this chupa I suddenly felt reconnected to Gila, as if she had sprinkled magical rose petals on me and pressed once more on the *Shabbat* **נפ̇ע** on my palm.

As we were dancing, I recalled Gila's enigmatic half promise, "If it comes about, there may come a time and I will give you something made by a famous person from long ago." And now, right now, at this moment, in the spin of the dizzying dance, just then the meaning of those slippery words became clear to me, supertitles write large on the screen of my febrile mind. I realized how un-enigmatic was her remark. How simple. How direct.

When I read Gila's line, with that big *If* and that conditional *may*, the weight of those two feathery words hung heavily on me, two monosyllables which determine to a degree man's fate. If you are good you may get rewarded. On the other hand, if you are good you may not get rewarded. Seeing that sentence I pictured what Gila might give me: a painting, an old coin, a handicraft, a poem, manuscript, book – obviously, something tangible. I never dreamt it could be reflexive.

Now, knowing what I knew—what I did not know then, when she wrote those words—now it was easy. It was Gila who was made by a famous person from long ago, Shlomo ibn Gvirol; and, if it came about, there may come a time and she would give herself to me. But when she wrote that veiled promise, how could I have known that she herself was made, and made by someone famous from long ago?

During this dance I watched Gila. A couple of times I noticed a tremor in her face and shoulders. She shivered, a quick shake of her head, as if an attack of palsy.

"I'm cold," she finally said.

And she shivered again, more noticeably this time.

At once I thought of Mazal shivering when she came in from the other room in my apartment around one a.m., and stood beside me in the dark that warm summer night because she was freezing, her body cold. And I fantasized that Gila too would come and stand next to my bed and I would bring her warmth, a kind of reverse of the Bible story when the lovely Avishag comes to King David's bed in the futile attempt to warm the cold, aging monarch.

"Come with me to the other room, Gila," Shlomo said. "I have something for you in my armoire."

As he said these words to Gila it seemed that I was saying them to her, "Come with me to the other room," or that both of us were saying them at the same time, just like some days ago, or was it more? Time in the interim had become indeterminate, for I couldn't tell if my first encounter with Mo had occurred five or fifteen days ago. For when I met him for the first time, we both uttered, remarkably, the same set of three words, and in the same order too, about the Great Synagogue of Venice: historicity, continuity and sanctity. Once more that disturbing frisson came over me, when I fantasized before that Shlomo might say to me, like out of an old-fashioned radio suspense drama: I am you. Was Shlomo ibn Gvirol an alter ego, or was I a latter day clone of this singular medieval poet?

Shlomo refolded the chupa and placed it on the floor. Then he added some words to Gila I barely understood, very likely in Old Spanish or Ladino.

As soon as they left the room a different ambiance overtook it. Was it Shlomo's doing, or was there an enchantment in that space that had nothing to do with him?

20   A Visitor

You know those sealed water-filled glass ovals about four-five inches high sold at tourist shops with tiny snowflakes falling when the glass is stirred? That's the scene that took place before me, writ large. But instead of snowflakes, in this big white-ceilinged room I saw letters from all the world's alphabets floating, thick as snowflakes. They reminded me of the rose petal shower in the attic but in many more colors, letters in Hebrew, English, Chinese, Greek, Arabic, Cyrillic, in a huge snowy display, swirling up, down, sideways, clockwise, rotating in a horizontal orbit like Saturn's rings, all of these movements together. I looked in vain for a word, phrase, a message amid this alphabetic maelstrom. Not even a two-letter word. Had I taken a photo of this scene I would have had a great work of modern art.

Then a tunnel opened amid the whorl of letters.

A man stood there, dressed in the same period outfit he was wearing last time I saw him. I recognized him at once.

"It's me, Leone da Modena," he said.

"I know." Even unsummoned, Mod had come back.

"Were you expecting me?"

"Of course," I said, and I really was.

"So was I."

He looked down at the floor. "What's with the chupa? Who's getting married?"

"No one I know," I said.

"You know I'm a rabbi too."

"Sure, I know." I understood his hint. Had thought of it just a few minutes ago.

Then Modena drew near, took out of his pocket something that looked like a bent needle, a little hook. He lifted my left hand, and before I had a chance to say, "What are you doing?" he carefully inserted the hook into the fabric of my suit jacket just above my wrist. Then he stepped back, and began pulling with the hooked needle.

At the periphery of my vision rotating still were the letters I had seen before. As I emerged from this carousel I realized the fabric of my jacket was unraveling. The hook Modena had inserted was the reverse of a sewing machine; instead of stitching it was un-stitching, and it did its work quickly. Before I could react, my jacket had become one long dark blue string. Like a fisherman, Modena was reeling in the threads of my suit. By now I was in my shirtsleeves. But that wasn't the end of it. I looked down and felt the fabric of my trousers starting to go, although I don't recall Modena hooking a needle into my pants.

In short, Modena had cast a spell over me. I was so dumbfounded I couldn't budge. And, worse, this unthreading had also reined in my tongue that could be as combative as Mo's. Now I understood why I had seen that huge swirl of letters in various alphabets. Modena had no doubt initiated that infinity of moving symbols as a camouflage.

I could only shout, "What's going on?" and, hearing no reply, after a pause I said, "Why are you doing this?" Even in confusion, surprise, astonishment, we still seek motive.

"I'm not doing. I'm undoing. You didn't keep your promise."

"But you're in the book. I showed you. And you've slipped into it even now. As we speak. And into the title too."

"But it's not because of your doing. It's because of my undo-ing." Modena stopped, evidently waiting for his words to sink in. Then he added, "And please note, I entered on my own, no thanks to you."

Now he was reeling in my trousers, waist, hip, pockets, thread by thread.

"Originally, I was supposed to be the hero of your story. And then you dumped me."

I stood there half naked. In shorts. I wasn't going to argue this point again. Then I had an idea. I figured maybe I could bar-gain with him. After all, his twenty-six trades, occupations and professions included selling amulets — I bet Mazal would have been a customer — practicing alchemy, doing dream divination, and dealing as a merchant.

"Let's talk," I said, using my best negotiating tone.

"Not while I'm doing my undoing."

"What else do you plan to undo?" I said with restrained cour-tesy. And I could actually feel the restraint pressing the lines in my furrowed brow.

And then, with his dumb reply, Modena undid himself.

"I'm going to unravel you, cell by cell, and then your book, letter by letter. First you, then your work."

That did it.

"You know what?" Now I shouted, and felt relief at that. The color of concern in my mind turned from stressed navy blue to relaxed spring-time green. "You can unravel my clothes, thread by thread, until I stand here naked as the day I was born."

"Not quite naked. Let's be precise. Grammarian/rhetorician is one of my professions too."

"Okay. Almost. Don't sidetrack me, Mod. And you can even

try to undo me. But my work, my story, my creation, that you won't touch."

My words, my outcry, did not move him. He put his right hand into the inside pocket of his purple doublet and showed me a little card, as if to prove his existence. It had the six-word title of the book you are now reading.

I made a quick sweeping motion with my left hand. The floating letters dancing around me vanished. Modena was still drawing in towards himself the threads of my clothing.

I tore off a piece of my thumbnail and with the jagged, sharp edge I cut the line of thread Modena was reeling in.

He staggered, reeled back, as if he himself were cut. I looked at my feet. Only the cuffs of my trousers were left. I stood there in my gray, quick washable shorts, long-sleeved white shirt, undershirt, socks and shoes. Last thing I saw was Leone da Modena running toward a door I hadn't seen before, holding that big bundle of thread. In my thoughts I reshaped it as a jacket and a pair of cuff-less trousers.

But that wasn't the end of it for, seeing that lonely chupa lying rag listless on the floor, I realized I wasn't properly dressed for a wedding and had second thoughts about letting him go. So I ran after and caught him, held his shoulders.

"This is no way for a groom to be dressed," I said calmly, catching my breath, as I drew with my right hand an imaginary line from my neck down to below my hips.

Modena stood there as if lifeless before me, rag doll limp, his aggressiveness going, going, gone. A look of defeat in his eyes, a look, had he gazed into a mirror, that showed the same aura of disappointment his eyes had seen in his lifetime during his countless unsuccessful labors and endeavors.

I took my ex-suit from him and placed it on the ground.

"Now it's my turn," I said, "but I don't need a bent needle or a little hook."

I went up to him, so close as if I were about to invite him to dance. Then I removed his purple doublet and put it on. It fit perfectly. "Next," I said. He knew what to do, for if he didn't do it himself, I would do it for him. He unbuttoned, stepped out of his pants, and handed them to me. I pointed to the thread bundle. He picked it up, then looked down at my cuffs.

"Oh, all right," I said and rolled the cuffs over my shoes. I suddenly felt sorry for this hapless man. "Here you are...You know, despite what you've done, I have no hard feelings toward you. I still like you and admire you. Do you know that I use your beautiful 1609 Venice Hagada every Pesach for the Seder?"

"You do?"

"In replica, of course."

"No matter. The originals are very rare. We only printed about two hundred copies."

"And I know of your sermons too here in the Great Synagogue. I read that the King of England's brother who attended a service here was so impressed with you he commissioned you to prepare an account of Jewish customs for his brother."

Leone da Modena smiled modestly.

"You are a very talented man," I added.

"Well, I earned my money with my pen, tongue and wits."

Then I stepped into his trousers, actually old-fashioned, rather ridiculous, wine-colored knickers. But what choice did I have?

"And this scene is going to be included too," I told him. "So you're going to be in the book even more than I had intended, despite you, you rascal, and despite me."

Gravely, Leone da Modena shook my hand, gave a courtly seventeenth-century bow and departed half naked, with undone dignity.

But, as he was leaving, he had time to say over his shoulders, in Venetian slang, "So why ain't I the full-fledged hero of your old-wives' tale?" before he disappeared.

Now I stood there, alone, waiting for Mo and Mu to return.

It did not take long.

21   The Chupa Dance — Which Will It Be?

As he came in, the first thing Shlomo said was, "I see you have changed too," but I don't know if he was referring to my attire or my personality. But Gila's remark was obviously about the way I dressed, for she said with a smile:

"Very fit for the era."

Now Gila looked comfortable. She wore a fetching green wool scarf around her neck and shoulders, which with a nimble move she threw gracefully around her head as if it were a turban, almost completely changing her appearance. Shlomo too, I now noticed, wore a jacket and an old-fashioned tie. And on his head, instead of a cap, was a round Bokhara yarmulke hand-stitched with various colors: bright red, green, orange and mauve, that extended like a hat without a brim to all sides of his head.

In the title of this brief history, this true narrative of my experiences in the Ghetto of Venice, I had called myself Me, and Gila, Mu (remember, it's pronounced "moo"), for at the beginning I knew her only as the mute beauty. Shlomo, obviously not wishing to reveal himself, went by the name Mo. Ma and Mod of course you know.

Shlomo picked up the wedding chupa again, gave each of us a pole, and the three of us, Me, Mu and Mo resumed the dance as if there had been no interruption.

As I was spinning around with Mu and Mo in this non-wedding wedding dance, the door that Leone da Modena had used opened and in came two more people. To complete my circle of Venice acquaintances, and add to the complications, entered Mazal, whom I had dubbed Ma, wearing an enticing tight-fitting, demure, short-sleeved, ankle-length, off-white dress (first time I'd seen her in a long dress, so formal looking. Was this a wedding gown?), and Rabbi Roni, Roni for short. Had Roni come to perform a wedding or to be married himself?

I couldn't tell if they had come together, or as Mazal had so deliciously expressed it in the Padua cemetery, "arrivey" — for I saw them in the equivalent of a wide screen devoid of sequential time. I don't know if Roni came first and then Mazal or if she had preceded him. Or if both had come at the same time. Because if both had entered together the story would have a different spin, page, angle, ending.

I couldn't take my eyes off Mazal, but I couldn't help see what she was carrying. In her right hand Mazal held a compact, pale grey portable typewriter, one of those slim, slick, lightweight models manufactured by the Italian Jewish family, Olivetti. What a quick turnaround for her! Not five days home in France and already she's keeping her promise of coming back to Venice and signaling she's ready to writetype my manuscript. On the one hand that was good news; on the other hand — perhaps it was my overwrought writerly imagination — it seemed to me, I can't say for sure, she was holding Roni's hand with her other hand, the hand that wasn't holding the handy Olivetti.

There are lots of hands here in the above line and that too added to my confusion. So if Mazal carried the Olivetti with her right hand and held Roni's hand with her left hand, she was sending mixed signals, maybe even a message that she was even-handed. Which is odd, for how anyone could be right-handed, left-handed, and even-handed at the same time was beyond me.

Mazal set the typewriter down by a wall and she and Roni joined the circular dance silently. Neither had greeted me. Maybe they didn't recognize me in my seventeenth century mode of dress. But they didn't greet anyone. Mazal remained silent, and Roni, most unusual for a rabbi, was silent too. And neither did Mu or Mo ask who the newcomers were. Nor did Mu nod to me after looking at Ma, as if to say, I thought she had gone back to Paris.

Now everyone held one mahogany pole of the chupa. Despite the five of us and four poles, each seemed to be holding a pole. And another puzzle. Whereas under the wedding canopy only one person — the bride — stands and the others parade around her, here, with all our swift movements, we seemed to move both within and without the circle, so it was difficult to tell who stood in the middle, as if our bodies had become diapharent, transaphanous, and everyone interwove with everyone else.

And so we danced around the invisible bride, all of us, rabbis and grooms, grooms and brides. A silent breeze coursed around about surround us, and although we had begun with three of us, Mo, Mu and me, holding up the four-sticked wedding canopy, when Ma and Roni entered and joined us, during our dancing the chupa hovered above us. In the distance sounds of a klezmer band, perhaps the guys from the Cafe Lavena come to honor me and play the traditional Jewish music they knew for the bride and the groom, even if it was hard to say who bride here and who groom, and even who the rabbi, for Roni was not the only one here with ordination. Remember? Shlomo was a rabbi too. But that still didn't explain how the chupa floated of its own accord, who would take the bride and who the groom, and who would be witness and who serve as rabbi in this room.

Leone da Modena did not come back; as a rabbi — matchmaker too was another of his many professions — Mod, the third rabbi in this room, could also have played a role here. In fact, I was half-expecting him to appear, officiate, and pocket a few ducats. No doubt he felt he wasn't dressed for the occasion.

Had Roni and Mazal come to my party, or was their presence here an invitation to come to theirs? But with Ma carrying the typewriter, wasn't that her promised return to me? Or was Mo's bringing out the chupa a sign that his long affiliation with Gila would now — now that she had gained that last important vestige of humanness: speech, and had become a full-fledged human being — would now take on a different shape and form, just like Gila had taken on a different shape and form? No longer was Gila the golem created by Shlomo to perhaps help serve the poet or keep him company when he was disfigured in face and depressed in spirit.

That song of love that Gila had sung — now I started looking at it in a different light — was perhaps just an awakening, not necessarily addressed to me. Behind Gila's poetic address was a mute message: you've awakened in me deep human feelings — for the man who fashioned me, the man I have been with and lived with all these years, even though in a mode you couldn't possibly believe or imagine.

Nevertheless, I wasn't sure. My imagination clouded everything. And imagination is not truth, just as poetry isn't truth and fiction isn't truth.

And even truth isn't truth.

At this point I didn't know what to do, what to write next. I closed my eyes, relaxed, took a deep breath, a breath so long and deep I thought it would never end. My lungs kept filling and filling till finally I decided to stop breathing in. On the screen of my closed eyes I saw a scroll, not like a megilla which, as you read it, unfolds horizontally, to the left, but a scroll that unfolded down from the top, like the one Leporello, in *Don Giovanni,* throws from one edge of the stage to the other listing his master Don Giovanni's conquests.

Before my eyes I saw the letters — again letters, but this time printed ones, no Technicolor floaty glyphs from various alphabets — and the words being created, but they moved so quickly I couldn't even make out one of them. It looked like a machine, an old-fashioned Linotype, pecking out letters with such speed I couldn't read them. The letters came out ivory on a dark grey background. The message was there. The answer to my unarticulated request: what to write next. Yes, it was as if an angel had come to my aid. But mystical intervention comes at a price. The scroll was turning so fast, top to bottom, the created letters and words just raced by. I saw only their shape, but their meaning eluded me. I guess angels only do speed-writing.

The story's denouement, then, was given to me; but the catch was — it played out in a tongue foreign to me.

So should I depict what I've seen and experienced, or should I conclude in a more writerly fashion? Embellish, adorn, enhance, sculpt, polish, edit. I was torn, here comes the old problem again, between truth and fiction — the seminal duel between the fiction of truth and the truth of fiction.

My eyes were still closed. I can't say I prayed, for what has God to do with creative writing? He had enough trouble putting together, with the help of editors like Ezra the Scribe, the entire Bible.

There were so many choices open to me, the fictionist, the creator, who has true freedom. As the famous Yom Kippur prayer has it, describing the clay in the hands of the potter, who expands or contracts the clay at will, so I too, a potter with words, can expand or contract, shape or reshape as I see fit.

I could end my Venice adventure with me going with Mazal, the poor French girl with religious and other problems, down to earth, sexy, sensuous and sensual, naive and openhearted, full of spunk, who did everything with passion. Or I could get Gila, the transformed woman, out of a mythic past, cooler and dignified, lovely in her own way, with an aristocratic grace, with long straight elegant fingers, who had cast an indelible mark, those three Hebrew letters for *Shabbat*, onto my body, perhaps onto my soul. That would be terrific, *n'est-ce pas*, me becoming an expatriate and ending up with an ex-golem   I see Modena casting a castigating grammarian's glance at me, and in my mind I amend it to *golemet*, to be precise in Hebrew and grammatically correct.

And the eyes of both of them, Ma and Mu. Three colors, if they stood side by side, plus some orange flecks. But shall I keep going, like the long and endless breath I took into my lungs before? Shall I summarize the qualities of each?

Both Mu and Ma called:

Me. Me. Me.

The three short

words I hear.

Which choice would please readers most? And me? And which would readers cheer? Like the two sides of the controversy in Mazal's synagogue that prompted her to come to Venice and search out the Master of Padua, only one could prevail. Obviously, whichever choice I made for my hero the other side would be disappointed.

Alternating with one and the other — in other words, having both — could not continue forever.

Lots of choices to be made.

One was Gila or Mazal. Mu or Ma.

The other, fiction or truth.

Or could we have, like in some fantastic mod operetta, a satisfactory menàge a trois?

Leone da Modena hadn't shown up to this operetta or Restoration comedy finale. I thought he would come, half-naked as I had left him. But there was yet another choice. I could have run off with Mod to a gaming table and asked him to draw a card for me that would determine the outcome. In other words I was contemplating precisely what I had criticized Mazal for during that wonderful Friday night dinner at Roni's house when I first met her. Relying on astrology, luck, fate, mazal, conjunction of stars. I was fantasizing, Let luck decide, not me. It would spare me an agonizing decision. Heart or diamond would be one; spade or club would be the other. If I drew a joker the joke would be on me and I would have run off to Venice with Modena and asked him to prepare me for the rabbinate. I was too live wire to submit to vows and take the veil.

When I opened my eyes I continued. Continued cogitating. And from the midst of my cogitation I hear a song, a chant, a poem, that I am singing and the four others are listening to, until the end. . . .

With five personae in the dance,
two are women, three are men,

you sense in less than one swift glance
that one must go, not why but when.

With a chupa there's a bride;
don't ask me who to whom is tied.
Regard the people in this room.
Can you point out the chosen groom,
and who the destined bride will be?
Will Ma or Mu now come to me?
Or Ma to Ron and Mu to Mo?
With chupa dance you never know.
No way to guess with endless spin
who is out and who is in.

The chupa round goes on and on.
See Mo with me and Mu with Ron,
Now Ron's with Mo and Ma with Mu.
Such dizzy turns are one neat trick
With me left by the chupa stick.

Then comes the cry, "Who's out? It's you."

Or maybe it should be read this way, more prosaically, with-out the distraction of the rhyme:

With five personae in the dance, two are women, three are men, you sense in less than one swift glance that one must go, not why but when. With a chupa there's a bride; don't ask me who to whom is tied. Regard the people in this room. Can you point out the chosen groom, and who the destined bride will be? Will Ma or

Mu now come to me? Or Ma to Ron and Mu to Mo? With chupa dance you never know. No way to guess with endless spin who is out and who is in. The chupa round goes on and on. See Mo with me and Mu with Ron. Now Ron's with Mo and Ma with Mu. Such dizzy turns are one neat trick with me left by the chupa stick.

Then comes the cry, "Who's out?...It's you."

But still it has the same effect, no matter poetry or prose.
Like in an unfair fight a punch in the nose.

I did not like this turn of events. Wouldn't, couldn't, accept it as the denouement to my tale. I looked at the four of them, that quartet that had sung the last line at me. But they returned my glance so beneficently — actually looking at me for the first time — and with such Schweik-like innocence, that for a moment I thought that that final choral judgment had come from elsewhere.

Could it have come from me, the architect of truth and deception?

I stared at Ma in that delectable tight-fitting dress, she was bursting out of it, and I swallowed. I remembered, tasted, on my lips, my tongue, my palate, all around the back of my throat, that long, loving kiss Mazal had given me when she rolled on top of me in my bed when she spent the night in my apartment and came to me on her own from her bed in the other room because she was freezing. And that ecstatic glissando loving between the tombstones in the Padua cementaire. And I looked at Mu and remembered, tasted, that taste hovering like a tiny sweet cloud in my mouth, that kiss tendered with all her heart, all her soul, all her might, that tour de force kiss, that kiss that was a first for her, that kiss that surely was the prelude, the inspiration for, the kiss that unlocked Gila's gates of speech.

And I decided that that eerie chorus was not going to command, commandeer, determine, my fate.

If indeed they chanted it.

And neither would words that perhaps I myself had unwittingly uttered — an example of downspirited dream speaking or automatic saysoothing.

I was the gondolier here and, standing tall, proud, aloof, I would, with a rhythmic balletic bend of my body and with noiseless dips and thrusts of my oar, I would decide where to go, which course to take.

No three or four words chanted at me like an incantation would tie my hands.

Nothing would stand in my way now.

Not reality.

Not truth.

Not fiction.

And now 1 shall begin to write the book I have just finished.

Curt Leviant

That is, to make a novel out of the true story I have just told.

Writing, in my left palm a glow, in my right a quill.

Curt Leviant

Curt Leviant is a translator and a fiction writer. He taught at Rutgers University. His novels have been published in eight European languages, in Israel, and in South America. His novel, *Diary of an Adulterous Woman*, was a best seller in Europe and was listed in France in 2008 as among the "Seven Best Novels of the Year".

Of his ten novels, the most recent are the critically acclaimed *King of Yiddish* and *Kafka's Son*. Critics have hailed the French translation of *Kafka's Son* and called Leviant "a worthy heir to Kafka." A Turkish version appeared in 2020.

His books have been praised by two Nobel Laureates, Saul Bellow and Elie Wiesel, and critics have compared his imaginative fiction to that of Tolstoy, Flaubert, Italo Calvino, Borges and Kafka.

His comic novel, *A Novel of Klass*, was chosen as one of the "Ten Best Novels of the Year in the USA" by Chauncey Mabe, the book critic of Florida's Sun-Sentinel. The same book critic, in reviewing another novel, wrote: "Curt Leviant is the best unknown novelist in America."

Curt Leviant's short stories have been included in Best American Short Stories and other major anthologies.